"Stay here tonight," he said, looking down at her. "Just stay here so we can figure this out."

Kate smiled, but shook her head. "Sex isn't going to solve anything."

"Maybe I just want you here," he retorted. "Maybe I've missed you, and now knowing that you're carrying my child, I want to take care of you."

The tenderness in his voice warmed her. She knew he'd want to take over and make sure everything was perfect for her. Unfortunately, through all of that, he just couldn't love her the way she wanted to be loved. The way she loved him.

Couldn't he see? This had nothing to do with the bar and if he kept it or sold it. If he loved her, truly loved her like a man loved a woman, she'd go anywhere with him. But she couldn't just uproot her life for a man who was settling and only trying to do the right thing.

"Stay," he whispered into her ear as he stroked her hair. "Sleeping. Nothing more."

She tipped her head back to peer up at him.

"Please."

* * *

RETURN TO STONEROCK:
In this small Tennessee town, neighbors
find the warmth of home...and love

Dear Reader,

Who doesn't love a good friends-to-lovers story? I knew from the moment I met Gray in *The Cowboy's Second-Chance Family* that he would need a special woman. He's infatuated with Kate but has never acted on his feelings. He's remained a faithful friend and a self-appointed protector.

Kate has had her share of heartache, and who better to lean on than Gray? She has her girlfriends, but Gray is different. She values their friendship and the special bond they've had since childhood.

But one night after their friends' wedding rehearsal changes everything. Suddenly they're more than friends...they're about to become parents.

I hope you enjoy Kate and Gray because I truly loved writing their story. Considering I married my best friend, I have a special place in my heart for this couple.

Happy reading!

Jules

From Best Friend
to Daddy

Jules Bennett

 HARLEQUIN® SPECIAL EDITION

Recycling programs for this product may not exist in your area.

ISBN-13: 978-1-335-46570-2

From Best Friend to Daddy

www.Harlequin.com

National bestselling author **Jules Bennett** has penned over forty contemporary romance novels. She lives in the Midwest with her high-school-sweetheart husband and their two kids. Jules can often be found on Twitter chatting with readers, and you can also connect with her via her website, julesbennett.com.

Books by Jules Bennett

Harlequin Special Edition

Return to Stonerock

The Cowboy's Second-Chance Family

The St. Johns of Stonerock

Dr. Daddy's Perfect Christmas
The Fireman's Ready-Made Family
From Best Friend to Bride

Harlequin Desire

What the Prince Wants
A Royal Amnesia Scandal
Maid for a Magnate
His Secret Baby Bombshell
Best Man Under the Mistletoe

Mafia Moguls

Trapped with the Tycoon
From Friend to Fake Fiancé
Holiday Baby Scandal
The Heir's Unexpected Baby

The Rancher's Heirs

Twin Secrets
Claimed by the Rancher
Taming the Texan

Visit her Author Profile page at Harlequin.com,
or julesbennett.com, for more titles.

Marrying my best friend was the best decision of my life. Love you, Michael.

Chapter One

"It's just one glass."

Kate McCoy stared at the champagne flute the best man held. He'd flirted with her all night during the wedding rehearsal dinner—and by her estimate in smelling his overwhelming breath, he'd had more than enough for both of them. Thankfully he was just Noah's cousin and visiting from out of town. As in, he'd be leaving after the nuptials tomorrow afternoon.

One of Kate's three best friends, Lucy, was marrying her very own cowboy, and Kate couldn't be happier. She could, however, do without Noah's cousin all up in her face.

"She doesn't drink."

That low, growly tone belonged to Gray Gallagher, her only male best friend and the man who always came to her rescue whether she needed him to
or not. She could've handled herself, but she wasn't
about to turn away backup since Bryan with a Y
wasn't taking her subtle hints.

Kate glanced over her shoulder and smiled, but
Gray's eyes weren't on her. That dark, narrowed
gaze was focused downward at the best man. Which
wasn't difficult. Gray easily had five inches and
an exorbitant amount of muscle tone on Best Man
Bryan.

"Oh, well." Bryan awkwardly held two flutes in
his hand, tossing one back with a shrug. "Perhaps I
could get you a soda or some water."

"We were just leaving," Gray growled.

He slid his arm around her waist and escorted her
from the dining area of the country club. Apparently
they were indeed leaving because he kept heading
toward the exit.

"I need to at least get my purse before you man-
handle me out the door," she said, swiping her clutch
off the table closest to the door, where she'd been
chatting with some guests. "And for your information, I was going to have a glass."

Gray stopped short in the hallway and turned to
her. "You wanted to have a drink with that lame guy?
You've never drank in your life."

Kate shrugged. "It's my thirtieth birthday."

"I'm aware of that." Eyes as dark as midnight narrowed. "You're not drinking with him."

Should she clue Gray in on her reasoning for wanting to have her first drink on her birthday and at her friend's wedding?

True, Kate hadn't so much as tried a drop of alcohol since her parents had been tragically killed in an accident. Her father had been thirty-five, her mother only thirty-two.

Now that Kate had hit the big 3-0, she'd started reevaluating everything about her carefully detailed life.

"C'mon." Gray slid his hand around her arm and escorted her out the door into the humid Tennessee heat. "If you're going to have a drink, it's not going to be with someone who can't handle champagne at a damn formal dinner."

Kate couldn't help but laugh. "That wasn't nice."

"Wasn't meant to be. I don't like how he looked at you."

What was up with this grouchy attitude tonight? Well, not just tonight. Gray seemed to be out of sorts for months now and with each passing day, he seemed to be getting worse and worse.

Gray headed toward his truck. He'd picked her up earlier and presented her with a box of chocolate-covered strawberries for her birthday. He knew those were her weakness and it was a tradition he'd started years ago when he'd first come back from the army only days before her birthday. Gray had told her he'd actually ordered her something this year, but it hadn't arrived yet.

"I'm picking you up for the wedding tomorrow, too."

Kate McCoy calculated everything, from matching her underwear to her outfit to the precise inches of curling ribbon she needed when wrapping packages. She had every detail in her life down to perfection and even owned a company that specialized in organizing the lives of others—everything from closets to finances. The Savvy Scheduler was still fairly new, but it was growing thanks to her social media accounts that drove interested viewers to her blog and ultimately resulted in many new clients.

Kate had anal-retentive down to a science. So she didn't like when her plans got changed.

"I'm driving myself in the morning."

Gray knew she calculated everything in her life well in advance. Hell, her planner had a planner. Everything in her personal life and business was not only on paper but also in e-format.

He was perfectly aware of how meticulous she was with every detail. They'd met in grade school on the playground when she made fun of his new haircut. Considering he'd hated it as well, they had a good laugh and bonded when other children would've fought over the mocking. They knew each other better than most married couples, which was why she couldn't pinpoint why he'd been surlier than usual tonight.

From scowling when he'd picked her up and muttered something about her dress, to the rude way he'd just escorted her out without saying goodbye to their friends, Gray's manners were seriously lacking.

"Plans change," he said with a shrug as he released his hold and walked ahead. "Relax."

Relax? The man had been uptight all night, glaring at any male guest who talked to her, but she was supposed to relax? What was up with him?

The wind picked up, threatening to blow her short skirt higher than was within her comfort zone and expose said matching panties. Kate fisted the bottom of her flare dress in one hand as she marched across the parking lot after Gray—which wasn't easy, considering she'd gone with three-inch stilettos for the special occasion.

Stubborn man. He always wanted to bicker, and tonight was apparently no exception. But his unexplained behavior was starting to wear on her nerves.

Honestly, though, she didn't have time to analyze Gray's snarly attitude. It was late and she was tired and sweaty from this damn heat. Coupled with the unforgiving humidity wave hitting Stonerock, she was becoming rather grouchy herself. What happened to spring?

"I *planned* on getting to the church early to make sure everything was ready for when Lucy got there in the morning." Why was she yelling at his retreating back? "Would you stop and listen to me?"

Gray didn't stop until he got to the passenger door

of his black truck. When he turned to face her, he released an exasperated sigh. He hadn't shaved for a few days, had that whole messy head of dark hair going on, and his tattoos peeked from beneath each sleeve that he'd cuffed up over his forearms. If she went for the dark, mysterious type, Gray would fit the bill perfectly. Well, also if he weren't her best friend.

Kate could easily see why women flocked to Gallagher's to flirt and throw themselves at the third-generation bar owner. He was a sexy man, had the whole "I don't give a damn" attitude, but she knew something those women didn't. Gray was loyal to a fault and didn't do flings. He may have looked like the quintessential bad boy, but he was all heart and a true Southern gentleman.

"Noah asked if I would bring you," he told her. "He said Lucy was worried about parking for the guests and he was trying to make things as simple as possible by having the wedding party carpool. I'll pick you up whatever time you want. Is this seriously something we have to argue about?"

One dark brow quirked and she thought for a scant second that maybe this was something they didn't have to argue about. Not that she was ready to concede the upper hand. First the angry attitude, now a lame argument?

"I'll pick you up," she stated, swiping away a hair that had landed right on her lip gloss. "I want my own vehicle there."

"Fine. Hop in." He motioned toward the truck. "I have to swing by the bar and get champagne out of the back stock since more was consumed tonight than originally planned. I'll give you a drink of whatever you want. But your first one will be with me."

"It's late, Gray. You don't have to do that. My list isn't going anywhere."

"List?" He shook his head, muttering something under his breath she couldn't quite make out. "Get in the truck. I should've known you'd have a damn list about taking a sip of alcohol."

Kate blew out a sigh. "I'm not sure, though. Maybe I should just mark it off and move on to the next item."

Gray reached out and tucked a strand behind her ear. "First of all, one drink of champagne or wine is a far cry from the ten empty vodka bottles found in the car of the person who hit your parents. Second, I'd never let you get in over your head. Third, what the hell is this list you keep referring to?"

The breeze kicked up, thankfully sending some relief over her bare shoulders, but making it impossible to let go of her dress. She'd left her hair down, which was a huge mistake. With that thick mass sticking to her neck and back, she'd give anything for a rubber band about now.

"It's silly."

"I live for silly."

Even without the dry humor, she knew Gray was as far removed from silly as any human being.

"Since I was turning thirty, I decided to make a list of things I want to do. Kind of a way to give myself a life makeover." She shrugged, because saying this out loud sounded even more ridiculous. "Trying a drink is on there."

"What else made the list?"

His eyes raked over her. Sometimes he did that. Like she was fragile. Just because life had knocked her down at times didn't mean she couldn't handle herself.

"Nothing for you to worry about."

She started to edge around him and reach for her handle when he stepped in her path. "Tell me."

Her eyes met his and she could tell by the hard stare that he wasn't backing down.

"I don't know what's up with you lately. You've been a bit of a Neanderthal." Might as well point out the proverbial elephant in the room. "You're pushy and hovering and…well, demanding. Just because some guy flirts with me doesn't mean I'm going to repeat old mistakes. And if I want a drink, I can do that for myself, too. I know you want to protect me, but you can't always do that, Gray. I'm a big girl and—"

In a quick move he spun her around and had her caged between the truck door and his hard chest. Mercy, he was ripped…and strong.

"Wh-what are you—"

"Putting that mouth to better use."

The words had barely processed before he covered

her lips with his. There was nothing gentle, nothing sweet or calm about Gray. He was a storm, sweeping her up before she even knew what hit her.

Wait. She shouldn't be kissing her best friend. Should she?

He touched her nowhere else and she still clutched her dress in one hand. On a low growl, he shifted and changed the angle of the kiss before diving back in for more. The way he towered over her, covering her body from lips to hips, made her feel protected and ravaged all at the same time.

Heat flooded through her in a way that had nothing to do with the weather.

Just as fiercely as he started, Gray pulled back. Cursing under his breath, he raked a hand through his already messy hair. Clearly he was waging some war with himself. Well, he could just get in line, because she had no idea what to do about what had just happened.

"Gray—"

"Get in the truck, Kate."

His raspy voice slid over her, making her shiver despite the heat.

What the hell did that mean? What did any of the past few minutes mean? Kate couldn't wrap her mind around his actions, his words. One minute she was trying to get to the bottom of his behavior and the next…well, she was being kissed by her best friend, and not just any kiss. No, he'd all but devoured her, almost as if he were trying to ruin her for another man.

Gray reached around her for the door handle, giving her no choice but to move. She settled inside and stared ahead, completely dazed. With his taste still on her lips and countless questions swirling through her mind, Kate didn't dare say another word out loud as she buckled her seat belt.

What on earth had triggered such an intense response? And then to just leave like that? She'd already told him that they couldn't be more than friends, but damn it, that kiss sparked something inside her she'd never experienced before.

Why did he have to go and do that to her? Why did he have to make her question her stance on their relationship and leave her aching for more?

More wasn't an option.

Chapter Two

The ride from the country club to Gallagher's had been too damn quiet. Tension had settled between them like an unwanted third party. Never before had things been this tense between them. They bantered, they bickered…that's just who they were.

But now, thanks to his inability to control himself, the dynamics had shifted completely.

Gray wasn't even going to question what had gotten into him. He knew full well that years of pent-up frustration from being relegated to the friend category, seeing her flirt and dance with other men at his bar and then being engaged and heartbroken, and finally that damn dress and heels tonight had all caused him to snap. There was only so much a man could take…especially from a woman like Kate.

And then the list. He wanted to know what the hell was on it and why she thought she needed to re-vamp herself. Not a thing was wrong with her. Who was she proving herself to?

Losing his cool and kissing her may not have been his finest moment, but every man had a breaking point and Kate McCoy had been his for far too long.

Damn, she'd tasted good and she'd felt even better all pressed against him. He wasn't sorry he'd kissed her, wasn't regretting in the slightest that he'd finally taken what he'd wanted. She'd leaned into him and obviously had wanted it just as much.

No, what angered him was the shocked look on her face and the fact he'd just pulled them both across a line they could never come back from. He was her friend, her self-appointed protector. She didn't have many constants in her life and she counted on him, damn it. She *trusted* him.

Now Kate stood at the bar, her eyes never meet-ing his. No doubt she was replaying that kiss just as he'd been over the past ten minutes.

Gray didn't say anything as he went to the back and pulled out a bottle of champagne that none of his customers would ever be interested in, but it was perfect for Kate. Once he got her home and came back, though, he was going to need something much stronger. Thankfully he could just crawl upstairs to his apartment after throwing one back.

Gray returned to the bar to find Kate exactly how he'd left her. He reached for a glass and carried that and the bottle around to the front side of the bar.

"I assume you still want that drink."

Finally, her blue eyes darted to his. "If anything in my life warranted a drink, this night would be it."

He poured her a small amount and slid the glass over to her. Kate stared at the peach-toned liquid for only a moment before picking it up and smelling the contents.

All of that long, dark hair curtained her face as she leaned down. With those creamy shoulders exposed, he was having a difficult time not reaching out to touch her.

Had he severed that right? Had he ruined everything innocent about their friendship when he'd put his lips on hers?

Damn it. He didn't like the idea of another man coming into her life. It had damn near killed him when she'd gotten engaged while he'd been in the army. Then, when the jerk had broken her heart, it had taken all of Gray's willpower not to pummel the guy.

Tonight he'd nearly lost it when Noah's best man had gotten flirty. Gray saw how Bryan looked at her, like she was going to be easy to take home. That wasn't his Kate. She didn't go home with random strangers.

Kate slammed her empty glass on the bar. "More."

He added a bit more to her glass and was a little

surprised when she tipped it back and swallowed it in one drink. Then belched like a champ.

"Wow. That's bubbly."

Gray couldn't help but smile. "It is. Had enough?"

"I can still taste your lips, so probably not."

His gut tightened as arousal spiraled through him. "Don't say things like that."

She lifted a slender shoulder. "Why not? It's the truth."

Gray took her glass away and set it aside with the bottle. The last thing she needed was to start buzzing, get all talkative and then regret spilling her secrets come morning. Though part of him—the part that had kissed her—would love to keep pouring and get her true feelings to come out into the open.

The low lighting behind the bottles lining the mirror along the bar wall sent a warm glow throughout the space. The main dining section and dance floor were still dark and Gray had never been more aware of a woman or his desire.

Over the years he'd purposely never allowed himself to be in a compromising situation with Kate, yet here he was only moments after plastering her against the side of his truck and claiming her lips.

"You can't be attracted to me," she murmured. "You *can't*, Gray."

If her words had any heat to them, if he thought for a second she didn't feel anything toward him, he'd ignore his need. But the only emotion he heard in her tone was fear and she'd kissed him right back earlier, so…

"You know I'm attracted to you." He closed the space between them. "I've never made it a secret."

"I'm the only woman who comes in your bar and hasn't thrown herself at you. I'm a conquest."

Anger settled heavily inside him. "Never call yourself that."

"Then what's the reasoning?" she tossed back. "Why me? After all these years, you're telling me… what? I need you to talk to me instead of being so damn irritated Why now?"

"Maybe I'm tired of seeing other guys flirt with you. Maybe I'm sick of you dating losers since your breakup because you know your heart won't get involved."

She'd been burned and her defense mechanism to set her standards low was slowly driving him out of his ever-loving mind. Couldn't she see that she deserved more? She should actually be expecting more.

"Why did you kiss me back?" he asked, shifting the direction back to her.

Gray adjusted his body to cage her in against the bar with one hand on either side of her hips. He didn't want her to dodge him or look away or find an excuse not to hash this out right here, right now.

Maybe it was the late hour, maybe it was the near-darkness surrounding them. Or perhaps it was just time that his war with himself came to an end one way or another.

Kate's eyes widened, then darted to his mouth. That innocent act had arousal pumping through him. His frustrating friend could stir up quite the gamut of emotions. One of the reasons he had always been so fascinated by her. Nobody could get to him the way she could. And nobody could match him in conversation the way Kate could.

She flattened her palms on his chest. "Gray, I can't lose you as a friend."

"I never said I was going anywhere." He leaned in just a bit closer, close enough to see those navy flecks in her bright blue eyes. Close enough for her to realize he wasn't messing around anymore. "Tell me you don't want me kissing you again."

Because as much as he worried he was pushing her, he kept returning to the fact that she'd kissed him back.

Kate's mouth opened, then closed. That was all the green light he needed.

Gray didn't waste time gripping her hips and capturing her mouth. Those fingertips against his chest curled in, biting into his skin through the fabric. She let out a soft moan as her body melted against his. He wanted to hoist her up onto this bar and see exactly what she wore beneath this damn dress that had driven him crazy all night. He wanted those legs wrapped around him, her body arched against his.

Kate tore her mouth away. "We can't... Why does this feel so good? It can't go anywhere."

Like hell it couldn't. She was just as turned on as

he was if the way she'd rubbed herself against him proved anything.

Gray slid his hands over the curve of her hips, to the dip in her waist, and back down. "Tell me to stop and I will."

He leaned in, trailing his lips over her collarbone, breathing in that jasmine scent that belonged only on her.

"Tell me, Kate," he whispered, smiling when she trembled beneath his touch. "I have to hear the words."

He was torturing himself. If she told him to stop right now he would. But damn it, being pulled away after having a sample would be hell.

Slowly her hands slid up around his neck, and her fingers threaded through his hair. "Gray," she murmured.

Music to his ears. He'd always wondered how his name would sound sliding through her lips on a whispered sigh. Now he knew...and he wanted more.

Gray hovered with his mouth right over hers, his hands circling her waist. "You want me."

She nodded.

"Say it."

"I want you," she murmured. "But I need you as a friend. Please. Tell me we won't lose that."

He didn't want to lose anything. He wanted to build on what they had. They couldn't ignore this pull between them, so taking this risk to see where things went was the only option.

When he said nothing, she eased back as much as she could with the bar at her back. "Gray, this night is all we can have. We'll still be friends come morning."

One night? Did she think she'd be done with him that soon?

"And nobody can know," she added. "I don't want Lucy or Tara to know."

Her girl posse. He understood the need for privacy, but at the same time, he didn't want to be her dirty little secret and he sure as hell wanted more than one night.

He was a guy. Wasn't he supposed to be thrilled at the idea of a one-night stand with no strings? He should've had her dress off by now.

But this was Kate and she was special. Always had been.

"I wondered."

Her words stopped every single thought. "What?"

Bright blue eyes came up to his. "About this. I wondered before."

"Kate," he growled.

"I mean it, Gray. Just this night and it stays here, between us."

There was so much he wanted to say, so much he wanted to fight for because Kate was worth fighting for. He'd worry about the semantics tomorrow. He'd come too far and had a willing woman in his arms right now. There was only one thing to do.

Gray lifted her up onto the bar and kissed her.

Chapter Three

Kate didn't want to think about why this could potentially be a disastrous idea. How could she form a coherent thought when her best friend had his mouth and hands all over her? She'd never felt this good in her life and her clothes were still on.

Was it the champagne? Surely not. She'd only had two small glasses

No, it couldn't be the alcohol. Gray was more potent than any drink he could give her. Why was she just discovering this fact?

Kate's head spun as she continued to clutch his shirt. She didn't want to analyze this moment or her emotions. She only wanted to feel.

Part of her wanted to rip off his clothes, but she'd

never been that brazen a woman. The few lovers she'd had were all calm, tame…and she'd never tingled like this for any of them.

She'd never ached with desire for her best friend, either, but here they were. A new wave of emotions swept her up, giving her no choice but to go along for the ride and enjoy every glorious moment.

Gray's firm hands rested on her knees as he spread them wide and stepped into the open space. He continued kissing her as his fingertips slid beneath her short skirt. Every single nerve ending inside her sizzled. When was the last time she'd sizzled?

Oh, right. Never. How did he know exactly what to do and how was she just realizing that her bestie had skills?

Kate tipped her head back as Gray's lips traveled over her chin and down the column of her throat. She circled his waist with her legs, toeing off her heels. The double thumps of her shoes hitting the hardwood floor sliced through the moment. Gray eased back and pinned her with his dark gaze. She'd never seen that look on his face before—pure hunger, passion, desire. All directed toward her.

Kate looked in his eyes and the need that stared back had her figuring maybe this wasn't a bad idea at all. No one had ever looked at her with such a need before. Something churned within her, not just arousal, but some emotion she wasn't ready to identify that coupled right along beside it, making her feel more alive and needed than ever.

Keeping his eyes locked on hers, Gray flipped her skirt up and jerked her by the waist toward the edge of the bar. Kate was completely captivated by the man before her. This passionate, sexual side of Gray had her reaching for the buckle on his belt, more than ready to hurry this process along. He quickly shoved her hands aside and reached for his wallet.

The second he procured a foil packet everything clicked in her mind. This was real. All of this was actually happening. She was about to have sex with her best friend…and she'd never been more thrilled, more excited in her life.

Shouldn't she be freaking out? Where had all of this come from? Clearly the desire had built up over time.

But she didn't. Kate waited, anticipation coiling through her. She'd address those questions later. Right now, she had a need, an ache, and judging by Gray's urgency, he did, too.

He tossed the packet next to her hip on the bar and unfastened his pants. Then, in a move that both shocked and aroused her, he reached beneath her dress, gripped the strip of satin that lay against her hip, and gave a jerk until the rip resounded through the quiet bar. So much for that pair of panties. They were a worthy sacrifice to the cause.

Kate didn't even get to enjoy the view before Gray sheathed himself and stepped toward her. With his hands firmly circling her waist, he nudged her forward once again, until he slowly joined their bodies.

Oh…my…

On a groan, Kate took a moment to allow her body time to adjust, but Gray clearly was in a hurry. He framed her face with his strong hands, tipped her head and covered her mouth as his hips jerked forward once again.

There was not much she could do but lock her ankles behind his back and match the perfect rhythm he set with their bodies.

"Kate," he muttered against her mouth.

She didn't want words. She had no clue what he was about to say, but she didn't want anything breaking into this moment. Words couldn't even begin to cover the tumultuous emotions flowing between them and she just wanted to feel. For right now, she wanted this man and nothing else.

Fisting his hair in her hands, Kate slammed his mouth back down onto hers. His hips pumped harder and in the next second, Kate's entire body trembled. She arched against Gray, pulling from the kiss. Her head dropped back, eyes shut as the euphoria spiraled through her.

She felt him lifting her before he settled her onto the bar. He whispered something just as his fingertips dug into her waist and he rose to tower above her. For a moment she marveled at his strength, but he started shifting again, moving faster and giving her no choice but to clutch his muscular arms.

Gray's body stilled as he rested his forearms on either side of her head, aligning their torsos. His mouth came down onto her shoulder. The sudden nip of his teeth against her flesh stunned her, arousing her even as she came down from her high. He kissed her there and trailed his lips across her heated skin.

Kate held onto Gray's shoulders even when their bodies completely stopped trembling. She had no idea what to say at this point. They lay on top of his bar half-dressed and had never so much as kissed more than in a friendly manner before, yet they'd just had explosive sex.

That was one hell of a birthday present.

Okay, maybe those shouldn't be the first words out of her mouth. But really, what was the protocol for a situation like this? She prided herself on always being prepared, but nothing could prepare her for what just took place. On a bar top, no less.

Gray came up onto his hands and looked down at her. Fear curled low in her belly. Was he waiting on her to say something and cut through the tension? Did they joke about this or did they fix their clothes like nothing happened?

Considering she analyzed everything from every angle, they would have to talk about this at some point. Maybe not right now when her emotions were too raw and she was still reeling from the fact that Gray had pursued her and torn off her underwear. Just the memory had chills popping up over her skin.

Exactly how long had he wanted her like this? There had been quite a bit of pent-up sexual need inside her bestie. Not that she was complaining. Definitely not complaining. Just…confused, and there were so many questions whirling inside her head, she had no clue where to start.

The muscle in Gray's jaw clenched and the way he continued to study her had Kate fidgeting. The top of her dress had slid down, so she adjusted to cover herself. She lifted onto her elbows and glanced around, anything but having to look right into those dark eyes to see…

She didn't know what she'd see, but she knew awkward tension had already started settling in.

Gray eased down off the bar and took a step back. Kate started to climb down, but he reached up, lifted her carefully into his arms, and placed her on the floor. The cool wood beneath her feet had her shivering, as did the sweet gesture of how he'd just handled her.

Of course, she could be shivering because her underwear was in shreds on the floor and her best friend was walking away. So much for him being sweet.

Apparently he wasn't one for chatter after sex, either. The silence only left her alone with thoughts she wasn't quite ready to tackle.

Kate's pale pink heels lay on their sides and she padded over to retrieve them. She clutched them against her chest like they could ward off the unknown, because she truly had no clue what was going to happen next.

Hell, it wasn't only the next few minutes she was

concerned with. What about long-term? Did this change everything between them? She hadn't been lying when she said she couldn't lose him. Gray was her everything. Absolutely everything.

The only constant in her life other than Tara and Lucy, but Gray was different. He was…well, he was special.

Right now, though, Kate could use some space to think and here on his turf, where her tattered panties lay mocking her, was not the place to clear her head and regroup.

Of all the times not to have her car. Damn it. This was why she always planned things, always had a plan B. But neither plan A nor B had been to leave the rehearsal dinner and have a quickie on the bar top at Gallagher's.

She was at the mercy of Gray whenever he came back and chose to take her home. Maybe then they'd talk and she'd get a feel for what was going on in that head of his.

Kate was stunned at the way her body still tingled. Gray had awakened something inside her, something she hadn't even known existed. But she'd made him promise just one night and that's exactly what she was going to hold on to.

She couldn't afford to lose him as a friend simply because she'd just experienced the best sex of her life. Gray was the one constant male in her life. He had been in that role since they were in junior high, and he'd come to rescue her from some bullying jerk who was new at the school. Not that she'd needed rescuing, but she'd appreciated it at the time, and he'd been her self-appointed white knight since.

So who was going to save her from him? Because now that she'd had him, Kate knew he'd ruined her for other men.

Gray Gallagher had infiltrated her, body and soul, and she'd better just live with the tantalizing memories, because they were definitely one and done.

She couldn't emotionally afford to have it any other way.

Gray took a minute longer than necessary in his private bathroom attached to the back office. The second he'd come back to reality and looked down into Kate's eyes, he'd seen her withdrawing. He'd instantly wanted her to reconsider that one-night rule. But he hadn't even gotten her completely undressed. He'd ripped her panties off, and they'd had a quickie on his bar.

Yeah, real smooth. Perfect way to show her she was special and he wanted to do it all over again. He'd be lucky if she didn't haul off and smack him when he walked back in there. Hadn't he always told her she deserved better? That she deserved to be treated like she was the most valuable woman in a man's life?

Gray slammed his hand against the wall and cursed himself for being such a jerk to the one woman he cared most about. Now he was going to have to go out and face her, make some excuse as to his behavior, and then drive her home in what he was sure would be uncomfortable silence.

What a fantastic way to end an already crappy day. He'd already been in a bitch of a mood when he'd seen that best man flirting with her. He shouldn't be jealous, but damn it, he couldn't help how he felt.

He'd faced death when he'd lost his mother at the tender age of five. He'd faced the enemy when he'd been overseas in the army. He faced his father, who was disappointed because Gray hadn't settled down and started a family. But Gray was not looking forward to facing his best friend, because if he saw even the slightest hint of regret or disappointment in her eyes, he would absolutely be destroyed.

Knowing he couldn't stay hidden forever, he made sure his clothes were adjusted before he headed out. The second he rounded the corner from the back hallway, he stilled.

Kate stood frozen just where he'd left her. She clutched her shoes, worried her bottom lip with her teeth, and stared at the spot where he'd taken her like some horny teen with no experience.

But it was the pale pink bite mark on her shoulder that had him cringing and cursing himself all over again.

Damn it. What the hell was wrong with him? His Kate was a lady. She was classy. She was so far above him and he'd treated her like a one-night stand.

Oh, wait. That's exactly what this was, per her

last-minute request. It wasn't like he gave her ample time to get used to the idea of the two of them together.

Still, Kate deserved better and he damn well was going to show her. Screw the one-night rule. If anyone should be proving to her exactly how she should be treated, it was him.

"I'll take you home."

Kate jumped and turned to face him, her eyes wide. His voice came out gruffer than he'd intended.

With a simple nod, she headed toward the back door. Gray didn't move from his position and ultimately blocked the opening to the hallway. He waited until she stopped right before him. He shouldn't touch her, shouldn't push this topic, but damn if he couldn't help himself. There had to be something he could do to redeem his actions.

Reaching out, he traced one fingertip over the faint mark on her shoulder.

"We good?"

Wow. He'd had several minutes to think of something tender, kind, and apologetic to say, and that's the best he could come up with?

Yes, he saw confusion looking back at him, but there was more. Kate wasn't upset, not at all. She had questions, of that he was sure, but she wasn't angry. Thankfully he hadn't botched this night up too much.

Kate attempted a smile. "We're good," she murmured as her eyes darted away.

She may not be angry, but she was no doubt wondering what they should do next. Kate planned everything and this whole experience had definitely not been planned.

Enter the awkward tension he swore wouldn't be there. He promised her they wouldn't change. He promised they'd be friends just like before.

Yet she couldn't even look him in the eyes.

"Kate."

Her focus darted back to him, but he didn't see regret. Kate's pretty blue eyes were full of desire... Damn if that didn't just confuse the hell out of him. She might be wanting to ask him about what just happened, but she also wasn't sorry.

Gray didn't know what else to say at this moment. The dynamics had changed, the intimacy too fresh. Maybe once they had some time apart and saw each other at the wedding tomorrow they'd laugh and joke and go back to the Gray and Kate they'd been hours ago.

Or maybe they'd find the nearest closet and rip each other's clothes off. Things could go either way at this point.

Gray moved out of her way so she could pass. Her hair hung down her back in dark waves, her dress was slightly askew, and she still clutched her shoes. He'd turned a moment of intimacy with his best friend into forcing her to do a walk of shame from his bar.

He was no better than the prick who'd cheated on her and broke her heart. But Gray would make this up to her. He had to.

Kate adjusted her one-shoulder bridesmaid's dress for the fifth time in as many minutes. Thankfully Lucy hadn't chosen strapless dresses. Kate needed this chiffon strap to cover Gray's mark. She didn't know what she would've done had he chosen the other shoulder.

Part of her loved the mark. She'd be lying if she said otherwise. She'd never had a man lose such control, and the fact he hadn't even been able to get them out of their clothes was thrilling. Sex should be thrilling, or so she'd heard before, and she'd always wondered if that was a myth. Now she knew.

Analyzing this over and over wasn't going to change the future. Gray wasn't going to happen again. On that they'd agreed, so now she had to figure out how to not compare any other man to her best friend. But at least the standards were set and she wasn't going to settle for someone who didn't at least give her a little spark.

Kate had definitely had a happy birthday. At least she had until he'd come from the bathroom and couldn't get her out of the bar fast enough. Did he regret what they'd done? Or worse. Was she a disappointment?

"Hey, you okay?" Tara whispered.

"Fine."

Kate smiled for the camera and hoped they were nearly done with all the photos. What did it matter if Gray found her lacking in the skill department? They weren't doing anything again anyway.

He'd barely said a word when she'd picked him up this morning and she hadn't seen him at the wedding. But the church had been packed, so that wasn't a surprise. She'd see him at the reception for sure. He was in charge of all the drinks and had brought a few of his employees to serve as waiters.

She felt a bit odd not sharing her epic, mind-blowing, toe-curling experience with Lucy and Tara. If this had been any other man she'd had wild sex with late at night in a closed bar, she would've texted them immediately after, but this was Gray. He was different and what they shared was...well, it was something she still couldn't describe.

"I think we got them," the photographer announced. "We'll do more at the reception."

Kate resisted the urge to groan. This was Lucy and Noah's day. She shouldn't be so grouchy, but smiling and posing and pretending to be in a good mood was not working for her. All she could think of was Gray: what they'd done, what she had missed from him that led up to that moment, how he'd react seeing her again.

Kate lifted the long skirt of her dress and stepped off the stage. A hand slid over her elbow.

"Wait a second," Tara said.

Turning her attention to her friend, Kate dropped her dress and clutched the bouquet. "What's up?"

"That's what I want to know."

Tara's questioning gaze held Kate in place. "I'm just going to hop on the shuttle to take me to the reception so I can get some food. I'm starving."

Rolling her eyes, Tara stepped closer. "You've been acting weird all day. What happened from last night to this morning?"

What happened? Oh, just a quickie on the bar top at Gallagher's, third stool from the left. Well, Gray had shoved the stool out of the way when he'd climbed up to her, but still. She'd never be able to look at that space again without bursting into internal flames. Her panties would probably melt right off.

"I just had a late night." Kate opted to go with some form of the truth. "Gray and I left the rehearsal and headed back to the bar so he could pull more champagne and wine from the back stock. I just didn't get much sleep before we had to be up and ready."

Tara's bright blue eyes studied Kate a moment longer than she was comfortable with. Gathering her skirt in her hand once again, Kate forced a smile.

"C'mon," she said, nodding toward the front of the church. "Let's go get on the shuttle so they can take us over to the food and dancing. I'm ready to get rid of these heels."

Tara nodded. "Will you get some pictures of me dancing with Marley?"

Marley, Tara's five-year-old daughter. She shared custody with her ex, Sam Bailey. Sam had brought Marley to the wedding since this was his weekend to have her. Tara had been surprised that Sam had taken Marley to get her hair done and her nails painted.

Kate knew Sam had some issues several months ago, but she saw the man was trying. Okay, using the word "issues" was really sugarcoating things. But addiction was such a delicate topic and Kate still wasn't sure how to approach it with Tara.

But Kate saw Sam fighting to get his family back. The man had gone to rehab, he'd gotten a new job, he'd gone to counseling. There was a determination in him now that Kate hadn't seen before. Tara wasn't ready to see it and Kate worried irreparable damage had been done and their marriage was over for good.

None of that was Kate's business and she had her own issues to worry about right now. Like seeing Gray at the reception. She didn't like the silence that had settled between them this morning. That wasn't like them. They were always bantering or arguing or joking about something. It was their thing. They lived to annoy the hell out of each other and for some strange reason, it worked for them.

Damn it. She knew sleeping with him would change things, but she'd been unable to prevent herself from giving in. One second they were friends, and the next he'd kissed her against his truck and made her want things she never realized she was missing.

Well, she had to just suck it up and get over this awkward hurdle. She wanted her friend back and she wasn't going to let great sex stand in their way.

Chapter Four

Gray checked on the status of the bottles, confident they'd be just fine with the extras he'd brought. He asked around with his staff to see if they were doing okay or if anyone needed a break. None of them took him up on his offer.

He had such amazing, loyal employees at his bar who would work any venue when he asked. Honestly, they could run the whole place themselves and probably didn't even need him around.

Damn it. He was out of things to do other than watch Bryan try to hit on Kate again. Didn't the guy take the not-so-subtle hint from the rehearsal dinner?

Gray had been jealous last night, but seeing him make a play again tonight had him feeling all sorts of rage. Which was absurd. Kate was a grown woman and they were just friends. They'd slept together and now he was letting that incident cloud his judgment.

Actually, he didn't care. Kate was better than Bryan and Gray didn't like the way the guy kept looking at her.

Gray walked around the perimeter of the country club dining area and glared at Bryan as he stepped in behind Kate on the dance floor. What the hell was wrong with that guy?

Kate turned and glanced at Bryan, then shook her head and held up her hands as if to ward him off. Bryan smiled and reached out to touch her bare shoulder. Seeing that man's hand against Kate's creamy skin had Gray making his way across the floor.

The jerk stepped into her when a slow song started and the tension on Kate's face made Gray's anger skyrocket. He was sure his face showed his every emotion but right now he didn't give a damn who saw him or what others thought. He was putting a stop to this now.

"Go have another drink, Bryan. This dance is mine."

Gray instantly wrapped an arm around Kate's waist and took her hand in his. From the corner of his eye, Gray saw Bryan still standing there. Spinning Kate in a circle, Gray stepped on Bryan's foot and was rewarded with a grunt.

"Still there?" Gray asked over his shoulder.

The guy finally disappeared through the crowd of dancers.

Kate's eyes were wide, but Gray would rather she be uncomfortable with him than with some idiot who didn't know what a treasure Kate was.

"He's harmless."

Gray narrowed his gaze. "And I'm not?"

She merely tipped her chin in defiance. "I could've handled it myself."

Gray offered her a smile. "You always say that."

"Because I can."

"I'm aware." He spun her around again, keeping his firm hold on her. His Kate was extra prickly today. "But we haven't danced yet and I had a few minutes to spare."

Her eyes continued to hold his. "And what were you doing those few minutes you were glaring this way?"

Damn if she wasn't adorable when she was fired up. "Some people take a smoke break. I don't smoke, so I take a glare break."

Kate stared for another moment before she finally shook her head and let out a soft laugh. "You're incorrigible. You know that, right?"

A bit of tension eased from his chest at her sweet laugh. "It's only because I care and Bryan is not the guy for you. Not even as a dance partner. Hell, he's not even your drink provider."

Kate arched a brow. "So now you're screening my guys?"

Screening them? Hell, if that was a possibility he damn well would be first in line to sign up for that job. If he hadn't been overseas during her ill-fated engagement, perhaps he could've prevented her heartache. But Gray hadn't even met the ex because he'd come and gone while Gray had been serving. So, yeah, perhaps he was looking out for her. Isn't that what friends did?

"Maybe dancing with a guy like Bryan made my list."

Here she went with that damn list again. He'd like to see exactly what was on that thing.

"Tell me more about this infamous list."

He spun her around again, slowly leading the way toward the edge of the dance floor, where there weren't as many people. He found he didn't want to share Kate right now. He wanted to keep her talking, keep her dancing. Though dancing wasn't his thing, it was an excuse to get her in his arms.

He glanced around as he led her. He recognized many people from town. The St. John brothers and their wives were all dancing. Several other couples who frequented his bar were also dancing and having a good time.

Gray actually hadn't seen the bride and groom for a while, though. Perhaps they'd already slipped out once the bouquet and the garter had been tossed. Most likely they'd been in a hurry to get to their honeymoon.

"I'm keeping my list to myself for now," she replied.

Gray stared down into her blue eyes. She hadn't brought up last night and he wasn't about to, either. They hadn't wanted things to change between them, but the tension had become palpable and he wasn't sure how to erase it.

Eventually they would have to discuss what happened. Might as well be now, while he had her undivided attention. Maybe having everyone around would help ease the tension. If they were alone again and trying to talk, Gray wasn't so sure he could prevent himself from touching her again. Touching her now was safe, smart.

"About last night—"

Kate's eyes widened a fraction. "I need to find Tara," she said, breaking from his hold. "We'll talk later."

And then she was gone, leaving him all alone with a slew of couples dancing around him. Gray fisted his hands at his sides. He hadn't expected Kate to run. He hadn't expected their night to scare her away. She'd always been comfortable with him.

But then he'd turned into the guy who had sex with his best friend on top of a bar.

Raking a hand through his hair, Gray left the dance floor and went back to what he could control. The alcohol and the servers. Right now, Kate was utterly out of his control. Perhaps they needed space. Maybe she needed a breather after what had happened.

One thing was certain, though. He'd had her only one time and he knew without a doubt he wanted more.

Kate sank onto the chaise in the seating area of the women's restroom. She slid out of her heels and resisted the urge to moan. Between all the food she ate and dancing and the lack of sleep, she was ready for bed.

It was that whole lack of sleep—or the reason behind it—that had her escaping to the restroom to hide for a bit. She'd known Gray would bring up their situation, but their friend's wedding was sure as hell not the place she wanted to hash things out.

She couldn't think when he was holding her, because now that they'd been intimate, any type of touch triggered her memories…not that the images of last night had ever faded to the background. Would they ever?

Besides, Kate had no clue what she wanted to say anyway. Did she say thank you? Did she compliment him? Or did she broach the fact that she'd had her first taste of alcohol and it wasn't that bad? What exactly did she lead in with after such an epic, mind-boggling night?

The bathroom door opened, but Kate kept her eyes in her lap, not wanting to face any guests.

"Who are we hiding from?"

So much for not facing anyone.

Kate glanced up to see Tara and Lucy holding the skirts of their gowns and coming in from the madness and noise outside. Once the door shut, her friends waited for her answer in silence.

"Tara—"

"Is it Bryan?" Lucy asked, rolling her eyes. "I swear, he and Noah are close, but I had no idea how annoying that man could be when presented with a single woman. Guess he thinks he has a chance with you."

Kate blew out a sigh. If her only problem involved a man who was a complete goober and found her attractive, she'd be golden and certainly wouldn't be hiding in the bathroom.

No, her issues came in the form of a six-foot-four-inch bar owner who could make her tingle just from the slightest brush of his fingertips.

"This isn't about Bryan. I'm just taking a breather," she told them, which was the absolute truth.

Lucy gathered the full skirt of her wedding dress and flopped next to Kate on the chaise. Tara crossed and sat in the floral armchair.

"I told you something was up," Tara stated, looking at Lucy.

"This is her wedding day." Kate glared at her friend. "You told her you thought something was up with me when she should be focusing on how quickly she and Noah can get out of here and head to their honeymoon?"

Tara's eyes widened as she shrugged. "We're friends. She can go have sex with Noah whenever. I need to know what's going on with you and Gray."

"Are you two arguing again?" Lucy asked. "I swear, you're like an old married couple, just without the sex."

Kate nearly choked on the gasp that lodged in her throat. Fortunately, she recovered before giving herself away. She was nowhere near ready to spill her secret. Her friends would be completely shocked if they learned she'd had sex with Gray. Kate was still reeling from the fact herself.

"What? No, we're not arguing." They couldn't argue when she was running away and dodging the issue. "Why would you think that?"

"Because you two were dancing, then you rushed out in the middle of the song."

Kate stared at Tara. "I didn't see you on the dance floor."

"I wasn't there. I was getting Marley another plate of fruit and dip when you scurried by," Tara explained. She pinned her with those bright eyes. "I'd assumed you were running from Bryan, but I saw Gray's face as he watched you."

Oh, no. *Damn it.* Kate didn't want to ask what emotions Tara had seen on his face, what feelings he'd been unable to mask. She honestly had no clue what he was feeling because he'd been so good at keeping that to himself since last night.

Of course, if she'd waited to hear what he had to say, maybe she'd be better in tune with what was happening in his mind.

"He stepped in and saved me from Bryan. You know how Gray is," Kate explained, smoothing down her chiffon-overlay skirt. She had to convince them there was nothing more than what was on the surface. "We just danced a few minutes until Bryan was gone. That's all."

Silence filled the room, which was good because the door opened again and an elderly lady came in. Kate didn't know her, but she'd seen her on the groom's side during the ceremony. Considering Noah wasn't from here, it would make sense that there were guests Kate didn't know.

"Would you go back out to your husband?" Kate hissed. "I'm just taking a break from those killer heels. Nothing is wrong."

Lucy took Kate's hand and squeezed. "Promise?"

"Of course." Kate nodded. "Go on."

Lucy finally got up and left. Once the other guest left as well, Kate was alone with Tara and her questioning gaze.

"What?" Kate demanded. "Can't a girl just take a break?"

"Lucy can and I can, but not you." Tara crossed her legs and leaned back in the seat. "You are always on the go, always planning the next thing, and I've never seen you relax. So what's really going on? And don't lie. I'm done with lies."

Kate swallowed a lump of guilt. Tara had been dealt too much lately, but there were just some things Kate wasn't about to share. That was not a reflection of their friendship. She'd tell her and Lucy... someday.

"Not now, okay?"

Tara's curiosity quickly turned to concern. "Promise me you'll come to us if you need anything. I know what it's like to be lost in your own thoughts and worry what to do next."

True story. Tara and Sam were going through hell all while trying to keep their daughter out of the fires.

"Same goes." Kate reached over and took her friend's hand. "Sam looked like he was doing really well."

Tara nodded. "He is. He left me a note on my windshield this morning."

How could anyone not find Sam and his handwritten notes simply heart-melting? He'd done that when they'd been married and since their split, he continued to leave her notes. Tara always mentioned them and Kate wondered what it would be like to have a man who cared that much.

The man was a hopeless romantic who'd just made some bad choices. Kate didn't blame Tara for being cautious, though. Some obstacles were just too great to overcome.

"We should get back out there." Kate came to her feet and stared down at her heels. "If I ever get married, we're all going barefoot."

Tara laughed as she stood up. "Deal."

Kate had pushed marriage thoughts out of her head long ago when her engagement ended. The whole ordeal had left her a bit jaded, but seeing Noah and Lucy come together after they'd both experienced such devastation in their lives gave Kate hope. She wanted to marry one day, to have a husband who loved her, start a family and live in the picturesque mountains of Tennessee.

One day, she vowed. But first she was going to have to figure out how to get back on that friendship ground with Gray. Every time she thought of him now, she only remembered him tearing off her underwear and climbing up on that bar to get to her.

And her body heated all over again. She had a feeling the line they'd crossed had been erased. There was nowhere for them to go that was familiar and comfortable because they were both in unknown territory.

Chapter Five

Gray slid another tray of glasses beneath the bar. For the past five days he'd gone about his business and mundane, day-to-day activities. This wasn't the first time, and wouldn't be the last, that he couldn't shake the void inside him. Something was missing, had been for quite some time, but he'd never been able to quite place it.

His father always said it was a wife and children, but Gray didn't believe that. He wasn't looking to settle down and worry about feeding a relationship. His parents had been completely in love up until his mother's death when Gray had been five. He'd seen how the loss had affected his father, seen how the man had mourned for decades. Gray didn't want to subject himself to that type of pain.

Besides, he'd never found anyone who would make him even think about marriage.

He'd been hand-delivered this bar when he'd come home from the army, just like his father before him. Gray's grandfather, Ewan Gallagher, had opened the doors when he'd retired from the army after World War II. Right after that, he'd married the love of his life and started a family. Same with Gray's father, Reece.

They'd both had a plan and been the happiest men Gray had ever known. Not that Gray wasn't happy. He knew how fortunate he was to have served his country and come home to a business with deep familial roots and heritage. Some men never came home, and some guys who did weren't even close to the men they'd been before they were deployed.

But beyond all of that, something inside him felt empty. The void that accompanied him every single day had settled in deep and he had no clue how to rid himself of it.

Gray pushed those thoughts aside and headed to the back office. He needed to get his payroll done before they opened this afternoon.

He sank into his worn leather office chair and blew out a sigh. He couldn't even lie to himself. It wasn't just the monotonous life he led that had him in a pissy mood. He hadn't seen Kate once since she'd deserted him on the dance floor.

They'd texted a few times, but only about safe topics.

Safe. That word summed up Kate. She did things by the book. Hell, the book she carried with her was like her lifeline to the world. She always had a plan, excelled at making her life organized and perfect.

Gray was anything but organized and perfect. He ran a bar. Things got messy and out of control at times. He'd obliterated her perfect little world when he'd taken their relationship to an entirely unsafe level.

Still, he was going to let her hide for only so long.

"Hello?"

Gray stilled at the unfamiliar voice coming from the front of the bar. He came to his feet and rounded his desk. He always left the doors unlocked while he was here working. Stonerock was a small town where everybody knew everybody. Crime was low and people usually respected his bar's hours.

Sometimes his buddy Sam would stop in during the day to talk or just to unwind. After all that man had been through, Gray wasn't about to lock him out. Sam needed support now more than ever and if he was here, at least Gray could keep an eye on him and be part of that support team.

"Anyone here?"

Definitely not Sam. Gray had no idea who'd decided to waltz right into his bar in the middle of the morning.

He stepped from the back hall and came to stand

behind the bar. The man who stood in the middle of Gray's restaurant clearly had the wrong address. Nobody came in here wearing a three-piece suit and carrying a briefcase. Who the hell even owned a suit like that? Nobody in Stonerock, that was for damn sure.

Gray flattened his palms on the bar top. "Can I help you?"

The stranger offered a toothy smile and crossed the space to the bar…third stool from the left. Now his favorite place in the entire building.

"You the owner?"

Gray nodded. People came in looking for donations for schools, ball teams, charity events…but Gray couldn't pinpoint exactly what this guy was nosing around about.

"My name is Preston Anderson. I'm from Knoxville."

Preston Anderson sounded exactly like the type of man who'd own a suit as confining and stiff as this one. Gray eyed the man's extended hand and ultimately gave it a quick shake.

"I have enough staff," Gray replied. "But the bank might be hiring."

The guy laughed and propped his briefcase on a bar stool. "I'm here to see you. I assume you're Gray Gallagher."

"You would assume correctly."

He pulled a business card from his pocket and

placed it on the bar. Gray didn't even give it a glance, let alone touch it.

"My partner and I are looking to buy a number of properties here in Stonerock and doing some minor revamping of the town."

Gray crossed his arms over his chest. "Is that so?"

"We'd like to make it a mini-Nashville, if you will. The area is perfect for day tourists to pop over to get away from the city, but still have a city feel."

Pulling in a breath, Gray eyed the business card, then glanced back to Preston. "And you want to buy my bar."

Preston nodded. "We'll make it more than worth your while."

He took a pen from inside his jacket pocket, flipped the card over, and wrote a number. Using his fingertip, he slid the card across the bar. Again, Gray didn't pick it up, but he did eye the number and it took every ounce of his resolve to not react. There was a hell of a lot of numbers after that dollar sign.

"You really want this bar," Gray replied.

Preston nodded. "We're eager to dive into this venture. We'd like to have firm answers within a month and finalize the sales within thirty days after that. All cash. Our goal is to have all of our properties up and running before fall for when the tourists come to the mountains for getaways."

Gray had never thought of selling this place before, and now he had a month to make a decision.

His initial reaction was hell no. This was his family's legacy, what his grandfather had dreamed of.

But reality kicked in, too. That void he'd been feeling? He still didn't know what was causing it, but all of those zeroes would go a long way in helping him find what was missing…or at least pass the time until he could figure out what the hell he wanted to be when he grew up.

Gray never had a set goal in mind. He'd done what was expected and never questioned it. But more and more lately he wondered if this was really where he was supposed to be. And if it was, then why did he still feel like something was lacking?

Preston went on to explain they'd still keep the establishment a bar, but it would be modernized for the crowds they were hoping to bring in. Gray had no idea what to say, so he merely nodded and listened.

The figure on the untouched card between them spoke more than anything Preston could've said.

"So, think about it," Preston stated, picking up his briefcase. "My number is on the card if you have any questions. This isn't an opportunity that will present itself again, Mr. Gallagher."

"I imagine not," Gray muttered.

Preston let himself out the front door, leaving Gray to process everything that had happened over the past ten minutes. He reached for the card, turning it from front to back.

What the hell did he do with this proposal? True, he'd never actually wanted the bar, but it was his.

And while he may have wanted to pursue other things in his life, there were some loyalties that came with keeping up tradition. Gray would never purposely go against his family.

Family was absolutely everything to him. His father never remarried, so Gray and his dad had been a team. Then Gray's grandfather had passed only a few years ago, leaving Gray and his father once again reeling from loss.

Now that they were all each other had, this business deal wasn't going to be something easy to say yes or no to. This was definitely a decision he needed to discuss with his father. But Gray wanted to weigh his options and have some idea of what he wanted before that discussion took place.

Gray already knew where his father would stand on this from a sentimental standpoint, but his father also didn't know that Gray hadn't been happy for a while now.

Ultimately, the final decision would belong to Gray.

There was one other person he wanted to talk to. One other person who'd been his voice of reason since junior high, when she talked him out of beating the hell out of some new jock who had mouthed off one too many times.

Sliding Preston's card into the pocket of his jeans, Gray went back to working on the payroll. Kate had one more day to come to him…and then he was going to her.

* * *

Kate's color-coded binder lay open to the red section. The red section was reserved for her most important clients. Not that all of them weren't important, but some needed more attention than others.

Mrs. Clements was by far her best client. That woman wanted help with everything from organizing her daughter's bridal shower to setting up her new home office. Kate also had a standing seasonal job with the middle-aged lady when it was time to change out her closets for the weather.

Kate stared at the time on her phone. It was nearly two in the morning, but she wasn't the slightest bit tired. This plan for Mrs. Clements wasn't due for nineteen days, but Kate wanted it to be perfect before she presented it to her.

Pulling her green fine-tip marker from the matching green pouch, Kate started jotting down possible strategies. The definite plans were always in blue and those were already completed and in the folder.

Kate tapped on her phone to fire up her music playlist before she started compiling a list of possible caterers.

The knock on her door had Kate jumping in her seat. She jerked around and waited. Who would be knocking on her door in the middle of the night? Probably some crazy teenagers out pulling pranks. But the knock sounded again, more determined than just a random tap.

She contemplated ignoring the unwanted guest,

but figured murderers didn't go around knocking on doors. Plus, this was Stonerock. She knew the entire police force. She could have anyone over here in a flash if something was wrong.

Kate paused her music and carried her phone to the door in case she needed to call upon one of those said officers. Of course Noah was still on his honeymoon with Lucy, so he wasn't an option.

As she padded through the hall, Kate tipped her head slightly to glance out the sidelight. Her heart kicked up. Gray. She knew it was only a matter of time, but she certainly didn't expect him in the middle of the night.

This man…always keeping her guessing and on her toes.

Blowing out a breath, Kate set her phone on the accent table by the door. She flicked the dead bolt and turned the knob.

Without waiting for her to invite him in, Gray pulled open the screen door and stepped inside.

"Won't you come in," she muttered.

"Considering I rarely knock anyway, I figured you wouldn't mind."

She closed the door, locking it before she turned to face him. "And what on earth do you possibly need at this time of the night?"

"You weren't asleep. I saw your lights on."

No, she wasn't asleep, and he'd just come from the bar. His black T-shirt with the bar logo on his left pec stretched tightly across his broad shoulders.

She could never look at those shoulders the same way again, not after clutching them the other night as he'd given her the most intensely satisfying experience of her life.

Suddenly the foyer in her townhome seemed too small. She couldn't be this close to Gray, not with those memories replaying through her head. The memories that made her question everything and want more than she should.

Clearing her throat, Kate turned and headed to the back of the house, where she'd turned a spare bedroom into her home office.

Gray fell in step behind her. She went back to her cushy chair at her corner desk and spun around to see Gray fold his frame onto the delicate yellow sofa she'd found at a yard sale a couple of years ago.

"Why am I not surprised you're working?" he asked, nodding toward the organized piles on her desk.

"I couldn't sleep."

"There's a surefire remedy for that."

Kate stared at him for a moment before she rolled her eyes. "Did you seriously come here thinking we'd have sex again?"

Gray quirked one dark brow. He stretched his long, denim-clad legs out in front of him and crossed his ankles. He placed one tattooed arm on the armrest. Gray was clearly comfortable with this topic based on the way he looked at her, taking in her thin tank and ratty old shorts.

His gaze was anything but friendly. Well, it was friendly in the sense that he looked like he wanted to strip her out of her clothes again.

Wait. He'd never gotten her out of her clothes the first time. Perhaps that's why he was staring so intently. But he'd seen her in a bathing suit and he'd most definitely seen her lower half.

Boobs. Men always wanted boobs. It was a ridiculous thing she would never understand. Still, he continued to stare across the office as if he knew exactly what she looked like in her birthday suit.

Had he always been this intense? This potent?

Kate shivered and tucked one leg beneath her. "Why did you really stop by?"

"I missed you."

The way those words settled between them had Kate's breath catching in her throat. He said them so simply, as if the question were silly and it should be obvious why he was here.

They hadn't gone this long without seeing each other since he'd served in the army. She appreciated how he put himself out there and used complete and utter honesty.

Another reason why he was her everything. Gray never sugarcoated anything and had always been up front with her. Considering her ex had been so deceitful, having Gray in her life was refreshing and made her realize there were good men out there. This good man, however, just couldn't be for her.

"I missed you, too," she replied, because she

wanted to be just as honest right back. "I've been busy with the Savvy Scheduler, the blogs and the scheduling for upcoming giveaways, and then getting ready for the next Helping Hands meeting. With Lucy gone—"

"You're hiding from me."

She really was getting ready for the next meeting. Kate, Tara and Lucy all led a weekly support group that helped to uplift those hurting from loss. They'd all experienced it themselves on some level, so it was a labor of love.

But perhaps she was using her work and the group to hide from Gray. Still, she'd always made time for him before and he'd never pushed her away. Not once.

Fine. So maybe she wasn't being totally honest with him, but how could she be when she was trying to fumble around with her own emotions and figure it all out herself?

Kate glanced down to her lap and stared at her pale pink polish. "I don't know what to do now."

Silence settled in the room. She had no clue what he was thinking, no clue how to get them back on the comfortable ground they'd been walking on for years. How could one moment undo years of friendship? How did sex muddle so much?

When the awkward tension became unbearable, Kate turned slightly and started straightening her desk. There had never been awkwardness between them and she desperately needed to rid this moment of it. She needed her Gray back—her best friend back.

She glanced at the outline for her next week and mentally tried to prepare herself and focus. At least this was something she could control, because she sure as hell couldn't control her feelings—not now that he was in her house and staring at her as if he wanted an encore bar performance.

No. No more sex—at least not with him. She shouldn't pay attention to her body when it started getting all revved up again at just the sight of Gray. She shouldn't keep remembering how he'd felt as he'd joined their bodies. And she sure as hell shouldn't keep wondering if there was any man who could measure up to him.

"We do what we've always done, Kate."

She shivered as his soft words pierced the silence and washed over her. Leave it to him to find a simple resolution to their tension. Maybe he didn't have the juxtaposition of feelings running through him like she did. Maybe he slept just fine at night and hadn't given her or their encounter another thought.

Kate slid the green marker back into the pouch, set Mrs. Clements's folder in her desk organizer labeled Things to Do, and worked the corners of the rest of the folders until they were perfectly lined up. Now what? There was nothing else to straighten or fiddle with.

"Look at me."

Oh, that low, sultry tone. Now that they'd been intimate, she could appreciate it so much more.

Kate gritted her teeth and spun around in her chair. That piercing stare had her gripping the edge of her chair. Anticipation curled low in her belly at what he would say or do next. She'd never been on the edge of her seat with him before.

Honestly, sex changed everything. Hadn't she warned herself about that in the few moments between the kiss and the torn underwear? But her hormones had taken over and Gray had been all too convincing...and she was human.

"We're still Gray and Kate," he reminded her, pinning her with that dark gaze. "We annoy each other for fun. We watch old movies and argue over the classics. I still worry you're going to choose another loser, so I'm extra cautious and overprotective. Yes, we had sex, but we're still us."

He made things sound so simple and easy, as if sex hadn't changed a thing. But it had changed everything. She found herself looking at him differently, seeing him in a completely different light. Because for a short time he'd been not only her best friend, but also her lover.

"That's why you came?" she asked.

"You didn't think I'd let you hide forever, did you?"

Kate smiled. "I would've been at Ladies' Night this week."

That side grin flashed over his face. "You missed last week, so I wasn't sure."

Kate picked at one of the threads on the edge of her shorts. "I just needed some space."

"Had enough?"

She chewed the inside of her cheek. "Maybe."

Gray came to his feet and crossed to her. He took her hands and pulled her up against him. Kate tipped her head back to look him directly in the eyes. A punch of lust hit her faster than she'd expected. She'd hoped that need, that ache, had vanished or had been all in her mind. But no. Gray had crossed the line and had settled deep into a place inside her. And she had no clue how to categorize him.

"You're done hiding or running, or whatever the hell else you were doing." He flashed her that devilish grin. "I need you, Kate. We've been together too long to let anything come between our friendship. Can we just get back there again?"

Something akin to relief slid through her at how easily he was putting them both back on stable ground. At the same time, though, she hated that they were going back to being just friends.

How could she just ignore how she felt now that he was this close? How could she forget how he'd kissed her? How he'd looked at her, touched her?

She couldn't forget. Gray had imbedded himself so far into her soul, she truly wasn't sure she could go back. She wasn't even entirely sure she wanted to.

"We are friends," she agreed. "You have to admit this is a bit awkward."

Gray laughed. "So stop making it awkward."

He pulled her into a hug just like he'd done for years. Only this time she couldn't prevent herself from pulling in a deep breath of that masculine scent, remembering how she'd been completely enveloped by that familiar aroma and the man. His potency had been all-consuming when he'd ripped off her panties and taken her on that bar top. Would she ever get that image, that *feeling* from her mind?

"You in a hurry to get home?" she asked into his chest.

"Not really."

Kate tipped her head back and smiled. "How about a movie?"

Gray kissed her forehead. "Perfect."

Chapter Six

"Tell me about this list."

Kate stopped tapping her toes on the side of his thigh. He sat on one end of the sofa and she had relaxed on the other, stretching those legs out, propping her dainty feet against his denim-clad thigh, and driving him out of his ever-loving mind.

Gray had known facing her would be difficult. Of course they'd seen each other at the wedding, but this was the first time they'd been alone and forced to really discuss what had happened at the bar. The tension still hovered between them, but he was going to push through because as much as he wanted her physically, he refused to lose her altogether.

Other than the obvious fact she'd been dodging

him, he knew she was panicking about where they were now. He knew she'd be trying to analyze things from every which angle and she wouldn't be able to. He'd wanted her for a while, longer than he probably wanted to admit even to himself, so there was no way she could decipher what the hell truly happened when he couldn't explain it himself.

For years, he'd been able to control himself out of respect for her and their friendship. Then, over the past several months, little by little, seeing her at the bar dancing with other guys, then at the rehearsal with Bryan, it had all just become too much and he'd snapped. Every man had a breaking point and she'd definitely hit his.

"It's nothing," she finally replied.

He curled his hand around her bare toes. "Tell me about the infamous list or I'll crack your toes."

Kate's legs jerked from his lap as she laughed. "Watch the movie and leave me alone."

"We've seen this at least a hundred times," he told her as he shifted on the couch to face her. He grabbed the remote from the back of the couch and muted the TV before tossing the device between them on the cushion. "Talk to me, Kate. You can't hide it forever. I'm going to get the truth out of you, you know."

She let out a sigh and shook her head. "Fine."

When she started to get up, Gray reached out and gripped her arm. "You don't have to go get some color-coded spreadsheet that no doubt you've laminated. Just tell me. I want to hear your words, not read some damn paper."

Kate smiled as she settled onto the couch. She swung her legs back up and he instantly started rubbing her feet. Maybe if she was relaxed she'd talk, and if she was talking about this mystery list, then perhaps he would focus on that and not the fact that he wanted his best friend now more than ever.

There was still the matter of discussing the business proposition with her, but right now there were much more important things to work out. It was just another area of his life he was confused as hell about. Once he talked to Kate and his father, he'd have a clearer picture of the future...he hoped.

"Tell me why you made a list," he started, needing to reel himself in from his wayward thoughts.

Kate adjusted the throw pillow between her head and the arm of the couch. Tipping her head sideways, she stared down at him. "My thirtieth birthday just passed."

"Yes, I'm aware of that." His thumb slid up over the arch of her foot. "So, what? You think you're old now that you're thirty? I'm thirty-one. We're barely getting started."

She smiled, which is exactly the response he wanted. He loved seeing that smile, loved knowing he could get such a quick, heartfelt reaction from her.

Lacing her hands over her abdomen, Kate blew out a deep sigh. "I don't think we're old. My mom was only thirty-two when she died, which was way too young. I just… I don't know. I guess I've been thinking too much over the past year. My mom probably thought she had her whole life ahead of her with raising me. Maybe she even wanted more kids. I have no clue. All I know is I don't want to lose out on anything because I was too busy working or assumed I had more time."

Gray's hands stilled. Her words hit hard. She was absolutely right. What if he kept up his day-to-day life, wondering what else was out there, what he was missing out on? Life was fleeting and nothing was guaranteed.

Should he take that business deal? Should he accept the money and sell Gallagher's, finally moving on to fill that void? The possibilities for him would be endless and the money would allow him to fully explore his options.

But at what cost? Disappointment from his father and the unknown of what he'd do next or if he would even stay in Stonerock. The risk from either decision weighed heavily on him.

"You okay?" Kate asked, pulling him away from his thoughts.

"Fine." He switched to her other foot and circled back to her needs. He wasn't quite ready to express his own just yet. "Tell me what you've put on the list."

"You'll think I'm silly."

"We've already established I live for silly."

Kate rolled her eyes and laughed—music to his ears. "Well, I'd like to go camping."

Gray couldn't help but laugh. "Camping? What in the world brought that up?"

"I don't know. It's just something I haven't done." She stretched her legs and rotated her ankles before dropping them back to his lap. "I live in the mountains, for crying out loud, and I've never been camping."

"So you made a bucket list?"

She nodded. "I titled it My Life List."

"Of course you gave it a title. What else is on there?" he asked, resting his hands on her legs.

"I'd like to get a dog and name her Sprout. A kennel dog or a stray. I can't handle the thought of all those abandoned animals while people are paying for novelty pets. It's heartbreaking. So I'll start with one dog. Who knows how many I'll end up with."

Someone as passionate and caring as Kate would want to help the less fortunate. Just another aspect he'd always admired about her. She was always looking at how to spread her light, even when she didn't always shine it on herself.

Kate kept her eyes on his as she discussed the items from her list. "I want to go to the beach since I've never seen the ocean. I'd love to throw a *Great Gatsby*–themed party and dress up and have fun all night. I think I'd like to go on a road trip. Of course I'd have to have it mapped out, but I want to just take off in the car and visit some national landmarks.

Once I get closer to checking that one off the list, I'll make a spreadsheet."

As he listened to her, Gray realized her goals were all so obtainable and there was no reason she couldn't do those things.

"I wanted to try alcohol, so that box is already ticked off," she added.

"In bright blue marker, I'm sure."

She reached up to swat his shoulder. "No, smarty-pants. Yellow is clearly the only choice."

Gray couldn't help but laugh. Kate took her feet from his lap and crisscrossed them in front of her on the cushion.

"So what else do you have?" he asked.

"I want to do something utterly spontaneous."

Gray stared at her, waiting for her to smile or give some hint that she was kidding. But she merely stared at him, completely serious.

"Darlin', you do realize you're missing the whole point of being spontaneous if you put it on a list and schedule it."

She toyed with the frayed ends of her shorts. Gray couldn't help but watch her movements, torment-ing himself further as he stared at the white threads lying against her tanned skin. He wanted to run his hands up those shapely legs. He wanted to strip her and have her right here on this couch.

Being together in the middle of the night with nothing around to interrupt them was probably not the smartest idea, but he couldn't bring himself to leave. He was dead-tired now, but she was talking. They were getting back to a place of comfort and familiarity. And she wasn't trying to make excuses for the mistake they'd made.

Only having sex hadn't been a mistake. It had been perfect and he was hell-bent on making sure it happened again. But above all, he didn't want her to worry about the future of their relationship. He'd never let anything—including his all-consuming desire for her—jeopardize that, because he needed her just as much.

While he respected her stipulation that their one night of passion stay just that, he wasn't going to let her ignore the attraction. If the opportunity arose again, if she gave the slightest hint she wanted more, he'd be all over it…and her.

"Well, I don't know what the spontaneous moment will be," she explained. "So it's not completely ridiculous that I listed it. I just want to try to be more… I don't know. Like you. You're so laid-back and carefree. I don't even know what that would feel like. But it's a short-term goal."

He wasn't going to state the obvious of the spontaneity on the bar. She'd probably already labeled that under something else.

"If you say so," he chuckled. "Anything else on the list?"

"Well…"

She was driving him crazy. "What? You want to

jump out of a plane? See the Mayan ruins? Take an Alaskan cruise? Just spit it out."

"Jump out of a plane?" She jerked back. "First of all, I wouldn't pick something so predictable, and second of all, hell no."

Gray laughed and curled his hands over her toes. "Tell me or I start cracking."

"I want to trace my heritage."

Intrigued at her statement, he relaxed his hands and stared over at her. "Seriously?"

Kate nodded and tipped her head to the side, resting on the back of the couch. "With my parents gone, I just want to know where I came from, you know? I don't have any other family and I was just a teen when they passed. It's not something I ever thought of asking them about."

Gray had never thought of that before. His grandfather had died only two years ago, but his father was alive and well and more than willing to pass down the family stories that could trace all the way back to their roots in Ireland. Kate didn't have anything like that.

While Gray had lost his mother at a young age and always had that hole in his heart, he couldn't imagine how Kate felt, essentially alone other than having friends. But that wasn't the same as family. Nothing could ever replace parents.

She'd lived with her grandmother for a while, but ultimately she passed, too. Thankfully Kate was older when that happened.

"I want to know where I got the combination of black hair and blue eyes," she went on with a slight smile. "It's a little silly, I know, but I guess I just feel like I need those answers. Maybe I have family out there and a long-distance relative I can connect with."

Gray hated that lost tone. She'd never mentioned feeling alone before. She'd never talked like she was hurting. At least, she hadn't said as much to him. Of course, she suffered from her parents' absence. That was something she'd never get over. But he really had no idea she'd been longing to find out where she came from. Kate should have every opportunity to trace her family roots. He'd make damn sure of it.

As she went through her list, he realized that he wanted to be the one to experience those things with her. They were best friends. Yes, she had Tara and Lucy, but Lucy was newly married and Tara was still struggling with Sam and their own sordid mess.

Gray wasn't going to let Kate feel alone any longer. Hell, he'd already helped her knock trying alcohol off her list. The rest would be a joy to share with her.

"We'll do this together," he told her.

Bright blue eyes snapped up, focusing on him. "Don't be ridiculous. I wasn't hinting that I needed a partner. I wasn't going to tell anyone about this list. It's just something I'm doing for me."

"I don't plan on telling anyone," he replied. "Keep

all the secrets about it you want, but I'm not going to let you do this alone."

Kate stared at him another minute before swinging her feet to the floor. She grabbed the remote and turned the television off, then put it back on the table.

"I really should get to bed." She stretched her arms above her head, giving him a glimpse of pale skin between her tank and her shorts. "I think I'm finally tired."

Yeah, well, he wasn't. Well, he was tired in the sense that he needed sleep, but he didn't want to leave. He could sit here all night and talk with her like they had when they were younger, with fewer responsibilities. Besides, she couldn't brush him off that easily. She was running scared again. He'd offered to help and she flipped out, jumping off the couch to get away from his touch. How could she choose this over intimacy?

If they just went with the sexual pull, the undeniable attraction, it would have to be less stressful than what was brewing between them now. How could she not see that? Was she simply too afraid to face the truth?

An idea formed in his head, but he kept the piece of brilliance locked away as he came to his feet. He knew she was tired, so he'd go. But he was done letting her hide behind her fear of the unknown and what was happening here.

"You look like you're ready to drop."

Gray took in her sleepy eyes, her relaxed clothing,

and there was nothing more he wanted to do than to pick her up and carry her to bed…and stay the rest of the night. Maybe he would one day. Maybe she'd realize that the one time wasn't enough and she wanted more.

He had every intention of respecting her wishes to stay in the friend zone—but that didn't mean he wouldn't keep showing her how perfect they were together. There was nothing wrong with exploring what they'd started. Besides, he knew Kate better than she knew herself at times. She had analyzed that night from every different angle and their intimacy was never far from the front of her mind. He'd bet his bar on it.

Said bar might not be his for much longer, though. But she wasn't in the right mind-set to discuss the potential sale now, and honestly, neither was he. Tomorrow, he vowed. There was too much at stake no matter which way he decided to go. Both choices were life-altering and would change not only his entire world, but that of his father and the town.

Gallagher's had been the pride of three generations now. His grandfather had wanted to set down roots, to have something that brought people together, because he'd seen so much ugliness tearing them apart. Ewan Gallagher had started a tradition, one that the people in this tiny town had come to appreciate and rely upon.

Gray didn't want that niggle of doubt and guilt to sway his decision. He wanted to look at this from a business and personal standpoint, but it was so difficult when the two were so inherently connected.

He dropped an innocent kiss on Kate's forehead and let himself out the front door. Gray waited until he heard her click the lock back into place before he headed to his car.

He knew he needed to grab sleep, but as soon as he got up, he was putting a few plans into motion. Kate was about to check off more items on her bucket list and he was personally going to see that she accomplished exactly what she set out to do.

Morning runs sucked. They sucked even more when little sleep was a factor and really all she'd wanted was to run to the bakery and buy a donut the size of her face. And by run, she meant drive.

Kate took a hearty chug from her water bottle as she pulled her key from the tiny pouch on her running shorts. She'd ended up falling asleep on the couch after Gray left, then stumbled to her room at about six and climbed into bed. When she'd woken up for good at nine, Kate realized she'd slept later than usual, so she'd hopped out of bed and quickly headed out the door to get in her miles.

She hated running. But that was the only way she could enjoy her donuts and still fit in her clothes. Besides, the exercise was a great stress reliever…so were pastries, but whatever.

As Kate opened her front door, she heard a vehicle pulling into her drive. Kate glanced over her shoulder, her heart skipping a beat at the sight of Gray's large black truck. The thing was as menacing as the man himself. He might look like the quintessential bad boy, but he'd listened to her drone on and on about her bucket list all while rubbing her feet.

Damn it. Why did he have to be her best friend? He was the perfect catch for any woman…just not her. She couldn't—no, she *wouldn't*—risk losing him as a friend. If she'd jumped at her initial reaction after the great sex and ignored common sense altogether, she might have made a play for him. But he was the only stable man in her life. He'd filled that role for far too long for her to just throw it aside and take the risk for something more.

Even if she went for more, what would it be? Gray wasn't the type to settle down. In fact, she knew his father mentioned Gray's bachelor status quite often and Gray brushed the notion aside. He seemed just fine keeping busy with his bar. The man rarely dated and even when he did, he kept it all so private. He was definitely not someone looking for happily-ever-after.

Kate took another drink as she waited on the porch for Gray to come up her flower-lined walk.

"Didn't you just leave here?" she joked.

He glanced up, flashing that megawatt smile he didn't always hand out freely. Mercy, the man was too sexy for his own good, and now that she'd had a sample of that sexiness, she was positive no other man would ever measure up.

How did one encounter have such an epic impact? Kate had to push aside what happened. It couldn't have been that great…could it? Surely she was just conjuring up more vivid details than actually happened.

Or maybe not. Gray did in fact tear her panties off and climb up the bar to get to her.

"I feel like I did," he replied as he mounted the steps. "You're sweating."

Kate rolled her eyes. "That happens when I go for a run."

"Well, you have ten minutes to get a bag together." He hooked his thumbs through his belt loops. "And if you want to shower, you better squeeze it in that time frame."

Kate jerked back. "Excuse me? Pack a bag?"

A mischievous smile spread across his face. "We're going camping."

"What?" Shocked, she turned and let herself in her house, trying to wrap her mind around his announcement. "I can't just go camping right now. I have things to do."

Her planner lay on the table just inside the door. She fingered through the colored tabs until she landed on the red. Flipping it over, she quickly glanced at her mounting list—color-coded with her favorite fine-point markers, of course.

"You can see there's no time," she stated as Gray followed her in. She used the tip of her finger to tap on the upcoming days. "I have to finish outlining a bridal shower and start on a new client's vacation schedule. Then I have to try to come up with some way to fit in my neighbor, who swears her closets are full but won't get rid of anything. Same story with her kitchen, so at this point I'm afraid her entire house needs an overhaul. I also have eight online clients I'm working with who found me just last week through my social media sites and referrals."

"And do you plan on doing all of that today?" he asked, crossing his arms and leaning against the wall beside her.

"Well, no, but—"

"You're down to eight minutes, Kate. If you hurry, I can even swing by and get a box of donuts on our way out of town so we can have breakfast in the morning."

"That's a low blow," she stated, narrowing her eyes.

"You need a break."

She slapped her planner shut and faced him. "I can't go camping last minute. I'd need sufficient time to strategize and make a detailed list of all the things I need to take. Hell, I need to research *what* to take. I've never been, so I have no clue."

That smile assaulted her once again. Damn cocky man.

"You're in luck," he replied. "I have been multiple times so I have everything you need, minus your clothes and the donuts I'll stop and get on the road.

Look at it this way—you can check off two things on your list. Camping and spontaneity."

Kate shook her head and sighed. "I can't mark off being spontaneous when it was your idea."

And she still hadn't marked it in regards to the bar sex. That needed a whole other label of its own. How could something so life-altering be checked off so simply? No, that encounter deserved more respect than just a quick X by the words spontaneous quickie.

Gray pushed off the wall and started for the steps. "You'll want a pair of jeans for when we go hiking, plus shorts, maybe a swimsuit, comfortable shoes that can get wet. It gets cooler at night so grab a sweatshirt or something with sleeves."

Kate watched as he just headed up to her bedroom like she hadn't just laid out several reasons she couldn't go. Did the man ever take no for an answer?

Her mind flashed back to the bar as her body trembled with the onslaught of memories.

So no. No, he didn't.

And here she was, contemplating going camping? Being alone with him all night and not invoking how she felt when he'd touched her, kissed her. This was not smart. Not smart at all.

Kate headed for the steps, rushing up to her bedroom.

"You're not getting out of this," he told her before she could open her mouth.

He opened her closet and jerked a sweatshirt off

the top shelf. Two more shirts fell to the floor as a result and Kate cringed.

"You're messing up my system here, Gallagher." She crossed over and instantly started sorting the mess back into neat piles. "You cannot just start packing my bag."

He shot her a wink. "Does that mean you're cuddling up to me for warmth and skinny dipping? Hey, I'm game, but you might be more comfortable with clothes."

Kate blew out a breath and leaned back against her open closet door. "You're not going to let this go, are you?"

"Nope." He took a step closer to her, his eyes all serious now. Gone was the playful smile. "Listen, if I didn't push you into this, I'm not sure you'd actually do it. Making a list is one thing, but following through is another."

"I would do it," She felt the need to defend herself because, damn it, she would do it…at some point. "I don't know when, but I would."

He tossed the sweatshirt behind him onto her four-poster bed, then took her by her shoulders. "My truck is packed. I literally have everything we need: a large tent, food, supplies, blankets. I got Jacob to cover at the bar for me tonight. We'll be back late tomorrow evening."

Kate stared into those dark eyes and knew if anyone could help her check items off her list, it was this man. He'd clearly gone to great lengths to set this up for her and she'd be a terrible friend, not to mention flat-out rude, to turn him down.

He'd literally thought of everything and he stood before her, having rearranged his entire life for two days just to make her happy.

Kate's heart flipped in her chest. Gray always did amazing things for her, but since the sex, his actions had taken on a deeper, more intimate meaning.

"Fine," she conceded. "But step away from my neatly organized closet and let me pack. I don't trust you over there and I promise I won't be long. You swear we're stopping for donuts?"

"I promise." Gray leaned forward and wrinkled his nose. "I'll give you an extra five minutes to shower. You smell."

Laughing, Kate smacked his arm. "Get out of my room. I'll be down in twenty minutes."

Once he was gone, Kate closed her bedroom door and started stripping on her way to the shower. She dropped her clothes into the color-coded piles in her laundry sorter just inside her bathroom.

Gray Gallagher was slowly making her reconsider that whole one-night rule. For a half second she thought about packing some pretty underwear, but then snorted.

Seriously? Even if she was after an encore performance, they were camping. She'd never been, but she had a feeling lace and satin didn't pair well with bug spray and campfire smoke.

Kate stepped under the hot shower and mentally started packing. No matter how this trip went down, she had a feeling lasting memories would be made.

Chapter Seven

"I did it," Kate exclaimed, jumping up and down.

Gray glanced over to the tent she'd put together. He'd set everything out and given her instructions, and damn if she hadn't erected their tent like a pro. He knew she wouldn't give up, but she'd definitely gotten it done much quicker than he thought she would. He was proud of her.

This was by far his favorite campground, but the spot he usually chose had already been taken and he'd had to choose another. He found one closest to a hiking trail near his favorite areas in the forest. He couldn't wait to share all of these experiences with Kate.

"Looks good." Gray came to his feet and wiped

his hands on his pants. "The fire is ready if you want to roast some hot dogs for lunch."

"I don't recall the last time I had a roasted hot dog."

Gray rolled over another large log and stood it up on its end as a makeshift stool. He'd found several near the designated fire area, but set up only the two.

"We had one at the bonfire last fall," he said. "Remember the fundraiser for Drake?"

Drake St. John had been a firefighter who had encountered several issues with the then mayor. Drake had decided to run for office himself and ultimately won. Drake and his brothers were pillars in the community and Gray had happily voted for him.

"Oh, yeah." Kate picked up one of the roasting sticks and held it out for him to put the hot dog on. "So I guess that was the last time I had one."

"Then you're long overdue," he replied, getting his own roasting stick ready.

The crackling fire kept his focus on cooking his lunch….and away from the swell of her breasts peeking from the top of her fitted tank. He had no business going there. This was about Kate. He wanted this to be an easy trip, something where she could relax and just be herself, take a break from work and all those damn schedules. He was here to make sure she was taken care of, first and foremost.

Silence settled easily between them, but so much swirled through Gray's mind. Kate, their turning point, the bar, the possibilities…the unknowns came at him from every single angle.

He still hadn't spoken to his father about the proposal. There were pros and cons that Gray could easily see now, but there was no clear answer.

"I jotted down some things for us to do," Kate said after a minute. "I looked on my phone for area suggestions while you were driving and made a list—"

"I saw you. You just had to bring your planner, didn't you?"

Kate gasped and stared at him as if he'd just asked if the sky was purple. "Of course I had to bring it. How else would I know what to do? I can't keep all these places and a timeline of when to visit them straight without writing them down."

Shaking his head, Gray rotated the stick. "You can relax for a day, damn it. I've got the trip planned and details covered. We'll be fine. Chill."

"I'm relaxed," she argued. "Look at me. Cooking a hot dog over a fire, sitting on a tree stump, completely relaxed."

"Where's the planner?"

She pursed her lips and shrugged.

"It's beside you, isn't it?"

Kate blinked. "I don't know what you're talking about."

Gray pulled his charred hot dog from the fire and tested it with his fingers. Black and crispy on the outside, just the way he liked it.

"What would you do if you didn't have that colorful binder?"

"I'd be lost. This is my personal one. But I need both personal and business or I'd never be able to function."

He threw her a sideways glance. "You've got to be kidding."

Kate came to her feet and pulled her hot dog from the fire. "Why is that so strange? I have too much to remember so I just keep it all nice and neat in my planner."

"But that's just your personal one," he stated. "You still have one for work."

Gray pulled the pack of buns out and set them on the old picnic table before grabbing bottles of water from the cooler.

"This is supposed to be a nice, calm overnight trip," he reminded her. "We don't need an itinerary."

She took a seat on one of the benches and grabbed a bun. "I need a plan or I'm going to miss out on things. So, like I was saying—"

"You've got me." Gray threw a leg over the bench and took a seat. "I have plans for us so put your planner in my truck and forget about it until we start to head home."

Kate's eyes widened. "You're joking."

He stared across the table. "Do I look like I'm joking?"

"I don't like camping already," she muttered around a bite.

Gray couldn't help but smile. He was going to get her to relax if it was the last thing he did.

"After we eat there's a little place I want to show you."

"What do I need to wear?"

"You're fine the way you are."

She'd come down the stairs at her house freshly showered. Her hair had been pulled up on top of her head in some wet bun thing she sometimes wore. She'd thrown on a tank that fit her curvy body perfectly, and her shorts showed off those legs she kept toned and shapely by her constant running. Though she'd looked perfectly fine before she'd taken up that hobby. She'd started running after her jerk fiancé left. Gray never did figure out if she was using the exercise as a natural form of therapy or if she thought something was wrong with her body.

Kate was pretty damn perfect no matter her look or her shape…at least in his eyes.

They finished their lunch and cleaned up, making sure to burn what they could before putting the food back in a sealed cooler to keep the hungry animals away.

"We've got things to do that do not involve spreadsheets or strict schedules," he informed her. "I'll wait while you put your planner and cell in my truck."

Kate hesitated, but he quirked his brow and crossed his arms. Groaning, she picked up her things and put them in the cab of his truck before coming back beside him.

"Happy now?"

Gray nodded and turned to head toward the marked trail. He wasn't sure if this camping idea was the greatest or dumbest move he'd ever made. On one hand, at least he was getting her out of her scheduled shell and she was checking things off her list.

On the other, though, they would be sharing a tent. Which wouldn't be a big deal if they hadn't already slept together. He'd warned her not to make things awkward between them, so he needed to take his own advice.

Still, anticipation had settled in deep because he had no idea how the night would play out once they were alone lying mere inches from each other.

"How far are we going?" she asked from behind him.

"About a mile."

She came up beside him. "I could've skipped my run this morning."

"You could skip it every morning and be just fine," he growled.

He hadn't meant to sound grouchy, but she worried about her body when her body was perfect. Why did women obsess about such things? Confidence was more of a turn-on to him than anything. Kate had to know how amazing she looked. Damn that ex of hers for ever making her doubt it.

They walked on a bit more in silence before they came to the top of a hill. He reached for her arm to stop her. With careful movements, he shifted her to stand and turn exactly to the spot he'd been dying for her to see.

"Oh my word," she gasped. "That's gorgeous."

Gray looked down into the valley at the natural waterfall spilling over the rocks. "This is one of my favorite places."

She glanced over her shoulder. "How often do you come here?"

"Not enough. Maybe once a year."

"And you've never brought me?"

Gray shrugged. "I tend to come alone to recharge, plus I never knew you had an interest in camping."

Kate turned her attention back to the breathtaking view. "I didn't know I had an interest, either, but I'm starting to love it. There's not a worry in the world up here. How could anyone even think of their day-to-day lives when this is so…magical?"

Something turned deep inside him. He couldn't put his finger on it, but as he stood behind her, seeing her take in this sight for the first time, Gray knew he'd be bringing her back.

This one night out here with her wouldn't be enough. Just like the one night of sex wouldn't be enough. Kate was a huge part of his life. He couldn't just ignore this continual pull between them.

Gray had always loved being outside, there was a sense of freedom he didn't have when he was be-hind the bar or doing office work. Knowing that Kate might share this…well, he was starting to wonder just how right they were together in areas he'd never fathomed.

"Can we climb down there and get a closer look?" she asked.

"We can, but you'll want to change."

She turned back to face him. "Why?"

"There's a natural spring you can swim in."

Her face lit up and she smacked his chest. "Then what are we waiting for? Let's get to it."

She circled around him and started heading back down the narrow, wooded trail. Gray watched her go and raked a hand down his face. First camping alone and now getting her in a bathing suit. Yeah, this whole adventurous weekend was a brilliant idea... for a masochist.

Kate smoothed her wet hair back from her face as she climbed back up the shoreline toward the grassy area with a large fallen tree serving as a makeshift bench. She grabbed her towel from the tree and patted her face.

Pulling in a deep breath and starting to dry her legs, she threw a smile at Gray, who had yet to put his shirt back on.

How long was he going to stand there? They'd splashed in the water, floated on their backs, then chatted a bit while just wading. Thankfully the conversation had stayed light, mostly about the beauty of the area and its peacefulness. There was something so calming and perfect about it. Kate was convinced no problems existed here.

Gray had gotten out of the water several minutes ago but still wasn't making any moves to get dressed. And that was pretty much the only reason she'd gotten out. They needed to get back to camp so he could put some damn clothes on and stop driving her out of her mind. Those water droplets glistening all over his well-defined shoulders, pecs and abs. The dark ink curving over his shoulder. There wasn't a thing about her best friend that she didn't find attractive.

Yes. He was definitely driving her out of her mind.

Unfortunately, Kate had a feeling he wasn't even trying.

She pushed aside her lustful thoughts. Okay, she didn't push them aside so much as kept them to herself as she turned her attention toward the brooding man. Something was up with him, but it could just be the sexual tension that continued to thicken between them with each passing day.

"That was amazing," she stated, blowing out a breath and glancing toward the crisp blue sky before looking back at Gray. He said nothing, didn't even so much as crack a smile. "But I guess we can't stay here forever."

Kate tightened the knot on her towel and when she lifted her eyes back up, those dark, mesmerizing eyes were directed right at her. She couldn't quite decipher the look, but whatever it was had her clutching the knot she'd just tied.

"What's wrong?" she asked.

Gray wrapped his towel around his neck, gripping the ends in one hand. "I've had something on my mind I want to discuss with you."

Instantly, Kate stilled. The only major thing between them was the new state of their relationship that they hadn't fully fleshed out. They'd brushed it aside in an attempt to get back on safer ground.

Was he about to open the memory bank and dig deeper? Fine. She needed to just remain calm and do this. They had to hash it out at some point, and better before they fell into bed together than later, so to speak.

Gray sank down onto the large old tree stretched across the ground. Without waiting to see what he was about to say or do, she took a seat beside him.

"What's up?"

Gray rested his forearms on his knees and leaned forward, staring out at the waterfall. The way stress settled over his face, Kate worried something else was wrong. If he wanted to discuss the other night, he'd be more confident. Right now, Gray appeared to be…torn.

Kate honestly had no idea what he was going to say, but the silence certainly wasn't helping her nerves. *Was* there something else wrong? Had he actually brought her out here to tell her he was sick or dying?

"Gray, come on," she said, smacking his leg. "You know my anxiety and overactive imagination can't handle this."

"I had a visitor at the bar yesterday morning."

Okay, so he wasn't dying. That was good. So what had him so upset and speechless?

Kate shifted to block the sun from her eyes. She waited for him to go on, but at this rate it would be nightfall before he finished the story. Whoever this visitor was had Gray struggling for words. Either that or he was battling something major and trying to figure out how to tell her.

"He offered me an insane amount of money to buy the bar."

His words settled heavily between them, rendering her speechless as well. Sell the bar? Is that something he actually wanted to do? She'd never heard him mention wanting away from something that she'd always thought held so much meaning. What would his dad say? Had he even talked to his dad?

There were so many questions crammed into one space and she wanted all of the answers now.

"Are you selling?" she finally asked when it was clear he wasn't going to add more to his verbal bomb.

Gray lifted one bare shoulder and glanced over. "I have no idea. I never wanted the bar, it was just assumed I'd take it over. When I came home from the army, it was there, so I stepped into role of owner."

"What would you do without it?"

He raked a hand over his wet hair and blew out

a sigh. "I have no idea, but I've always wondered. I mean, with the amount I was offered, I could do anything."

"You haven't talked to your dad."

Gray shook his head, though she hadn't actually been asking.

"Is that why you brought me camping?" she asked. "So you could get my opinion?"

Gray reached for her hand. "No. I mean, I knew I wanted to talk to you, but the second you mentioned that list and started naming things off, I knew I was going to bring you here as soon as I could get everything lined up. It just happened to be rather quickly."

Kate couldn't help but smile as she glanced down to their joined hands. "Have you made a list of reasons to stay and reasons to go?"

His lips twitched into a grin of their own as he shook his head. "No, ma'am. I leave the list-making to you."

Her mind started rolling on all the good things about owning a family business. There was just so much, but only Gray knew what he loved most about the place.

On the downside, once you owned a business, you were married to it. Randomly he would take a day, like this, but the man was loyal and that bar was his wife, baby. Plus, he carried on the small-town tradition his grandfather had started.

Family heritage meant everything to someone like Gray. Money could only go so far. She was surprised he even considered selling the bar, which meant he must really be looking for something else in his life.

Kate's heart ached for him, for this decision. If she were in his place she wouldn't even have to think about it. She had no family and would kill to carry on this kind of legacy.

"Your silence is making me nervous."

Kate smiled and patted his leg. "You should be nervous. The pros and cons are already lining up inside my head."

Gray led her back to camp and she was somewhat grateful for the distraction. Though she didn't think anything could fully take her mind off the ripped torso covered with tats that he still hadn't covered. She'd be lying if she didn't admit her nerves had settled in at the thought of spending the night in that tent with him.

But first, she'd help him figure out what to do about this business proposition. Surely that would crush any desires…wouldn't it?

Yes, if they just continued to focus on the bar and his proposal, then any desires they shared would be pushed aside and they could reconfigure their friendship.

Kate would keep telling herself that until it became the truth.

Chapter Eight

The fire crackled, the stars were vibrant in the sky, and beside him, Kate continued to jot down notes. She'd mutter something, then mark out what she'd just written. Every now and then she'd ask him a question and scribble something else down.

Her system was driving him insane. She fidgeted, pulling her hair up into a knot, then taking it down and raking her fingers through it. Then she'd start the process all over again. Watching her was killing him, mostly because her mind was working overtime, but just seeing her in her element was too damn sexy.

Kate let out a groan. "I need my colored markers so I can see the overall picture clearer."

Gray had had enough. He reached over, jerked the planner from her lap and tossed it into the fire.

"Gray!" Kate leaped to her feet and stared down as the pages curled, turned black, and drifted up in ashes. "That was my personal planner. You can't just—"

"Too late. I just did."

Okay, maybe he should feel bad, but she needed to relax because until she did, he couldn't. She'd brought the damn thing camping when this whole night should be about taking a break from reality.

Now she sat here working on his life like he was one of her damn clients. No more.

"Not only does that have my whole life in it, I had the lists for you about the bar."

Kate spun around and propped her hands on her hips as she stared down at him. He picked up the long stick he'd had beside him and poked around at the fire, shoving the last bit of the planner further into the flames for good measure. It was better than seeing that snug little tank pulling across her chest or the creamy patch of skin between the hem of her shirt and the top of her pants.

"You're a jerk."

She stomped off into the darkness, heading toward his truck. Gray bit the inside of his cheek to keep from laughing. She most likely had a backup planner at home and he knew she kept duplicate electronic files. He felt only a little guilty. She'd be fine. Knowing Kate, she had everything logged into her memory bank anyway. Someone who was so focused on details and schedules and color coding the hell out of every minute of life would definitely know her schedule by heart.

The slam of his truck door had Gray glancing in that direction. Seconds later, Kate came stomping back with her cell in hand. She flopped back onto the fat stump she'd been using as her seat. The glow of her phone added a bit more light to their campfire area.

"You can't be serious," he grumbled.

Without looking up, she started typing like a mad woman. "Oh, when it comes to schedules, I'm dead serious. And even though you just ruined my life by burning my planner, I'm still going to help you work this out."

Gray tossed the stick back to the ground. "I'm not making a decision tonight, so relax."

"You keep telling me to relax, but if I don't worry about it and try to come to a conclusion, who will?"

Gray stood and took a step toward her. She jerked her phone behind her back and tipped her chin up in defiance.

"You're not throwing this in the fire," she said, and he thought he saw a ghost of a smile on her lips.

"No," he laughed. "But I'm not worrying and neither are you. I'm tired and it's late so I thought we could get our sleeping bags rolled out and get some rest. I want to get up early and hike to the top of the peak so you can see the sunrise."

"Sounds beautiful."

"Words can't describe it." Gray held out his hand to help her up. "So you may want to get some sleep or you'll be grouchy when I wake you."

"I'm grouchy now," she muttered, placing her hand in his. "You owe me a new planner, but I get to pick it out. I don't trust you anymore."

He helped her up, but didn't let go of her hand. "Now, where's the fun in that? You may love the one I choose."

"Please," she said, and snorted. "You have terrible taste. I've seen that painting over your sofa."

"Hey, *Dogs Playing Poker* is a classic. I paid good money for that."

"From a flea market, maybe," she muttered. Kate shook her head and blew out a sigh. "We better just go to bed and stop arguing."

Gray wasn't sure why he hadn't let her go, or why he continued to watch as the orange glow from the flames tinted her cheeks. Now her hair was down from the knot she'd been wearing. It had air-dried from the swim earlier...a swim that he took way too long to recover from. She'd only worn a simple black one-piece, but he knew exactly what she had hidden beneath that suit. She may as well have been naked. The V in the front and the low scoop in the back had been so damn arousing, he'd had to recite all fifty states in alphabetical order to get himself under control.

Gray kept hold of her hand, pulling it up to his

chest. Her eyes remained locked on his. Sounds from crickets filled the night, the crackling of the fire randomly broke into the moment.

"Gray," she whispered.

"Kate."

Her eyes closed as she pulled in a deep breath. "You're making this difficult."

"None of this has to be difficult," he countered. No reason to pretend he didn't know what she spoke of. They both had the same exact thing on their minds.

"No, it shouldn't be," she agreed, lifting her lids to look at him again. "But when I'm around you, I just remember the bar and how that felt. And then I wonder if my memory is just making the whole scenario better than it actually was."

Good. He'd been banking on her replaying that night, but he hadn't expected such an honest compliment. He sure as hell remembered, too, and not just when he was with her.

Even when he was alone or working, especially working, he recalled how stunning she'd been all spread out across the gleaming mahogany bar top. She was like a fantasy come to life.

There wasn't a doubt in his mind that she wanted him, too. He could see the way her gaze kept dropping to his mouth, the fact she hadn't let go of his hand, the way she'd avoided him for days after their intimacy. She was afraid of her feelings, of taking what she wanted.

"I don't expect anything once we go in that tent," he explained. The last thing he wanted was for her to think that was why he actually brought her here.

"I didn't think that." She licked her lips and curled her fingers more tightly around his hand. "You understand why I made the one-night rule. Right?"

She might need him to know, but that didn't mean he wanted to. All Gray cared about was how they felt, and ignoring such intense emotions was only going to complicate things further down the line. The resulting tension would eat away at their friendship and drive a wedge between them much more than taking a risk would.

"I can't lose you, Gray," she went on, staring up at him like he was everything in her life. "It would destroy me."

Kate had looked at him that way before, when her parents died and when he'd come home from the army. He didn't want to be some type of hero to anybody.

No, that wasn't right. He did want to be her hero, but not someone she thought needed to be on a pedestal. He wanted to be her equal, to prove to her that they were good together.

Fortunately, he didn't need to prove such things. She already knew just how good they were…and that's what scared the hell out of her.

"You're the only constant man in my life." She squeezed his hand. "Do you even know how important that is to me? Tara and Lucy are great, but they're not you."

Gray swallowed the lump in his throat. He didn't get emotional. Ever. But something about her raw honesty, her vulnerability got to him.

"You really think I'd let something happen to our friendship?" he asked, staring into her expressive eyes.

"Neither of us would mean for anything to happen to it," she countered. "But are you willing to take that chance?"

"I'd never risk hurting you," he stated. Gray palmed one side of her face, stroking his thumb beneath her eye. "You think I don't understand where you're coming from? You have to notice you're the only constant woman in my life basically since we met."

A smile played over her mouth. "You date."

"I do, but serious relationships aren't my thing. I'm too busy with work to feed a relationship or worry about a woman." He took a half-step closer until they were toe to toe. "I need this friendship just as much as you do, but I'm not going to ignore these feelings forever, Kate."

Her eyes widened. "You promised—"

"—that I wouldn't let you lose this friendship and that I wasn't pressuring you for anything tonight. But you can't run from your feelings forever. I won't let you deny your own feelings, either."

Unable to resist, Gray dropped a quick kiss on

her lips, not lingering nearly as long as he would've liked. After releasing her and taking a step back, he finally turned and headed to the tent.

This was going to be one long, uncomfortable night.

Kate rolled over in her sleeping bag for what seemed like the eighteenth time in as many minutes. Facing Gray now, she narrowed her gaze to adjust to the darkness and make out his silhouette.

How dare he throw down that gauntlet and then lie there and get a good night's sleep? How did the man turn his emotions off and on so easily?

She wanted to know the secret because this jumbled up mess inside her head, inside her heart, was causing some serious anxiety issues. As if she didn't have enough to handle where this man was concerned.

Kate couldn't make out his face in the dark. But she knew it by heart just as well as she knew her own. The faint lines around his eyes and between his brows gave him that distinguished look she found sexier than she should. His dark lashes always made the perfect frame for those dark as night eyes. She'd bet they were fanned out over his cheeks right now as he slept peacefully.

When he'd come home from the army, he'd been harder than when he'd left. Whatever he'd seen overseas had done something to him, something she never could put her finger on. But then he'd jumped right in and taken over the family business.

Some men came home a shell of who they'd once been. While Gray might be harder and more closed off to some, he was alive and thriving in their little town. He might not like the word *hero*, but he was hers. Honestly, he always had been.

Just another reason she couldn't keep exploring these new sexual feelings. The friendship was so, so much more important.

When Gray had implemented Ladies' Night at Gallagher's, the women around town had flocked there, all trying to catch the attention of the town's most eligible bachelor. Ladies from surrounding towns also came in to see the sexy new vet turned bartender.

Kate had always been aware of Gray's ridiculously good looks. She wasn't blind or stupid. She'd just never thought about acting on her attraction. She could be attracted to someone and still be friends… right?

Well, she'd been doing just fine at managing both until he propositioned her on the bar top. The sex couldn't have been as good as she remembered. It simply couldn't. And yet it was all of those overexaggerated flashes in her mind that had her all jumbled and aching now when she had no right to be.

"Are you going to stare at me all night?"

Kate jerked at Gray's mumbled words. He hadn't even cracked an eyelid open, so how did he know she was staring? Her heart beat faster at the abrupt break in the peaceful silence.

"I can't sleep," she answered honestly. No need to tell him her insomnia was due to him. Gray wasn't stupid.

"I can tell from all the flopping around you've been doing."

Now he did open his eyes. Even though she couldn't make out the color in the dark tent, she knew they were fixed on her.

"Sorry I kept you awake," she whispered, though why she was whispering was lost on her. Maybe because everything was so peaceful around them and she needed to hold on to that just a bit longer. Lately, so much in her life didn't seem calm. Well, maybe not so much. Mostly just Gray and their friendship, which trickled down to everything else because she couldn't stop thinking of him, of what had happened, and how to move on.

Gray shifted in his sleeping bag. When his knee bumped hers, a jolt shot through her. Being hyperaware of him in the middle of the night with these sexual urges spiraling through her was not good. Not good at all.

But there wasn't one thing she could do to stop how she felt. Why did these feelings have to be awakened inside her? How long had she had them and not even realized it?

Yes, she'd wondered if they could ever be more than friends. She'd thought of sex with him. He was hot. She was a woman. It was the natural order of things. But she'd always pushed those thoughts aside and focused on their friendship.

That wasn't the case right now.

"Your movement didn't keep me awake," he countered.

Kate curled her fingers around the top of her sleeping bag and tried to resist the urge to reach out. So close. He was so close she would only have to lift her hand slightly to brush the side of his face. She knew from firsthand experience exactly how that bristle would feel against her skin.

Kate swallowed. She shouldn't be fantasizing about that stubbled jaw beneath her palm. She shouldn't wonder if they both could fit into one sleeping bag. And she sure as hell shouldn't be thinking how quickly they could get their clothes off.

"What's keeping you awake?" he asked.

Kate snorted. "You're joking, right?"

"Do I sound like I'm joking?"

No. He sounded sexy with that low, growly voice she'd never fully appreciated until now.

"You've got me so confused and worked up," she confessed. "Why couldn't we just keep things the way they were?"

"Because attraction doesn't follow your rules."

Kate closed her eyes and chewed on her lip. What could she say to that? He was right, but that didn't mean she wouldn't keep trying to compartmentalize her emotions. They had to stay in the friend box.

They had to. Everyone in her life had a special area inside her heart, but Gray kept stepping out of his designated spot and causing all sorts of confusion.

"You're not the only one losing sleep over this, Kate."

Oh, mercy. Those were words she wished he hadn't thrown out there to settle between them. Not now, when they were being held hostage by the circumstances surrounding them. The dark night, the enclosed tent, the sexually charged energy that seemed to be pulling them closer together.

Her heart beating a fast, steady rhythm, she reached out. When her fingers found his jawline, she slid her hand up the side of his face. That prickle of his coarse hair beneath her palm had her entire body heating up.

"What if..."

She couldn't finish. This was insane. This entire idea was absolutely insane and not smart. But she ached...for this man.

His warm, strong hand covered hers as he whispered, "What if what?"

"One more time," she murmured. "We do this just once more."

"Are you going to regret it this time?"

Kate eased her body closer. "I didn't regret it last time."

He released her hand and jerked on the zipper of his bag before sliding hers down as well. In another swift move, he was on her, taking her hands and holding them on either side of her head.

"Tell me now if you want me to stop."

Kate arched against him, pulling against his hold. "Now, Gray."

Chapter Nine

The green light couldn't be brighter. And one time? Sure, he'd heard that before. Whatever. He'd take this time and show her again exactly how perfect their special bond was.

Gray eased up just enough to slide his hands beneath the long-sleeved T-shirt she had on. He hadn't been able to appreciate her before at the bar, and it was so damn dark he could barely see, but he was going to get her naked and not fumble around ripping underwear like some inexperienced, out-of-control teen.

With some careful maneuvering and assistance from Kate, Gray had her clothes off in record time.

His hands settled on her bare hips as she reached up to frame his face.

"You're still wearing clothes."

Gray gripped her wrist, kissed her palm and put her hand on his shirt. "Then take them off."

Her hands trembled as she brought them to the hem of his tee. She jerked the material up and over his head. When she grabbed the waistband of his shorts, he sucked in a breath. Those delicate fingers on his body might be more than he could handle. To say he was hanging on by a thread would be a vast understatement.

Since she'd paraded around in that swimsuit, he'd been fighting the ache to take her hard and fast. Gray covered her hands with his and took over. Within seconds, he was just as bare as her.

Kate eased her knees apart, making room for him. Her fingertips grazed up his arms and over his shoulders. "I wish I could see you better."

Gray reached over, taking the lantern-style light he'd brought. He flicked the switch on and left it against the edge of the tent. When he turned his attention back to Kate, his breath got caught in his throat. A vise-like grip formed around his chest.

She lay beneath him, all of that dark hair spread around her, her eyes bright and beautiful and solely focused on him.

"You're stunning."

He hadn't meant to say the words out loud. He'd wanted to keep this simple—or as simple as they

could be, considering their circumstances. But now
that they were out, he wasn't sorry. Maybe Kate
needed to hear this more often. Maybe she needed
to realize just how special and amazing she was.

A smile spread across her face. "I'm already
naked," she joked. "You don't need to flatter me."

If she wanted to keep things light, that was fine.
Having Kate here with him, like this, was more than
he thought would happen.

But he didn't want more words coming between
them. All he wanted was to feel this woman, to take
his time with her, and show her how much she was
treasured. Above all else, he never wanted her to
feel like she was just a one-night stand. Even if they
agreed to stay friends, he needed her to know she
was worth more than quick actions and meaning-
less words.

Gray covered her body. Then he covered her
mouth. Her delicate arms and legs wrapped all
around him.

"I need to get protection," he muttered against
her lips.

Her hold tightened. "I'm on birth control and I
trust you."

The whispered declaration had him battling over
what he should do. There was nothing more he
wanted than to have no barrier between them and
he trusted her, too. He'd never gone without because
there wasn't a woman he trusted that much.

But he knew his Kate and he wasn't about to move

from this spot, not when she was holding on so tight and looking at him like she couldn't take another second without his touch.

Gray settled himself between her thighs, bracing his forearms on either side of her face. He smoothed her hair back, wanting to see every emotion that flashed across her face when he joined their bodies.

And he wasn't disappointed.

The second they became one, her lids fluttered down, her breath came out on a soft sigh, and she arched against him.

Kate's fingertips threaded through his hair as she urged him down, opening for another kiss. How could he ever agree to just one time with her? Hell, he already knew that twice wouldn't be enough.

She muttered something against his lips, but he couldn't make out what. Her hands traveled down to his shoulders, then his back as she tossed her head to the side. Raven hair covered a portion of her face as she cried out, her legs tightening around him.

Gray shoved her hair out of the way, basking in the play of emotions. He'd never seen a more beautiful, expressive woman than Kate. His Kate. No matter what happened, friends or more, she'd always be his.

In no time he was pumping his hips, capturing her mouth beneath his. Kate's nails bit into his back and that was all he needed to send him over the edge. Nothing had ever felt like this…well, nothing except their encounter at his bar.

Gray held on to her, nipping at her lips as he trembled. After several moments, and once his body stilled, he gathered her close and pulled the open sleeping bag over them. He didn't care about their clothes, didn't care that there was a little chill in the mountain air. He leaned over with his free hand and clicked the light off.

"That was the last time," she muttered against his chest. "I mean it."

Gray smiled into the dark. He'd never agreed to that bargain to begin with.

"These new pamphlets turned out so nice."

Kate glanced to Tara, who was waving around the stack of brand-new promotional material for their grief center. Judging by the look on her face, she'd been talking for a while, but Kate had zoned out.

"What? Oh, yes. They're pretty. Lucy did a great job with the design and the colors."

They'd just had new pamphlets done a few months ago, but with the popularity of their weekly meetings, Lucy had taken it upon herself to design the new ones, adding some testimonials from the regulars and having nicer pages printed online.

"You're distracted," Tara stated, dropping the stack to the table at the entryway of the community center. "Does this have anything to do with the camping trip?"

Kate shook her head. "No. Gray and I just went away for a day. It was pretty cool. I can't believe

I live in this gorgeous state and have never taken advantage of the mountains. I'm definitely going camping again."

The waterfall had been amazing, but the sunrise only hours after making love had been something special. She wasn't sure where Gray's thoughts were, but for her, something had changed. She needed a breather and she needed to do some serious reevaluating of where she stood on her feelings for her best friend.

What had she been thinking, telling him not to use protection? Not that she didn't believe him that he was safe, but that bold move was, well…bold. They'd taken their intimacy to another level when she knew full well they couldn't do that ever, ever again.

But when she'd been lying beneath him, cradled by his strength and seeing how he looked at her, she simply hadn't wanted him to move away for anything. She'd wanted him and only him.

Besides, they were fine. She was on the pill and neither of them had ever gone without protection before.

"What's up with the two of you lately?" Tara asked.

Before Kate could answer, she was saved by the adorable five-year-old running around the tables and singing something Kate didn't recognize.

"Marley Jo Bailey," Tara scolded. "You cannot run in here. I brought your bag in and put it back in the kitchen. You have crayons, a coloring book and your new baby doll to play with."

Marley stopped at her mother's abrupt tone, or maybe it was the use of her full name. Either way, the little cutie started skipping toward the back of the building, where the kitchen was located.

"Sorry about that," Tara said, turning her focus back to Kate.

She wasn't sorry one bit. Marley's running got Kate out of answering the question that had been weighing on her, because honestly, Kate had no idea what was going on with Gray.

"Is Sam working?"

Tara nodded. "He's always good to keep her on meeting nights, but he got a new job and he's worried about asking off."

Kate smiled. "Sounds like he's getting things back in order."

"He left me another note."

"He wants forgiveness," Kate stated. "It's obvious he loves you."

Her friend nodded and glanced back toward the kitchen area. "I know he does. That's never been the issue."

Kate couldn't imagine what her friend struggled with. Between losing her husband to addiction only to have him fight and claw his way back, and having a sweet, innocent child in the mix...there was so much to take in and Tara was handling things like a champ.

"So, back to Gray."

Kate resisted moaning. There was no way she was going to offer up everything that had happened between them. She and Gray were still friends and that's what they'd stay, because the other night was it. No more taking her clothes off for her best friend.

"He's just going through some personal things right now and needed to escape and get some advice."

There. That wasn't a total lie. She'd offered him advice, hadn't she? She'd told him to take his clothes off.

"And you gave him advice?" Tara asked, her raised brows almost mocking.

"Well, I was trying to until he tossed my planner into the fire."

Something she was still pissed about, but seemed to have forgotten about the second he'd touched her and made her toes curl all over again. Damn that man for making her want things she couldn't have—and for destroying her beloved planner.

And in answer to her question from days ago, yes. Yes, the sex was just as fabulous as she'd remembered. Maybe more so since they'd both gotten out of their clothes this time. Gray had been rather thorough and her body continued to tingle at just the mere thought of how gloriously his hands had roamed over her as if memorizing every aspect.

"The fire?" Tara gasped, throwing a hand to her chest. "Tell me he didn't burn the cherished planner."

"Very funny." Kate playfully smacked Tara's shoulder. "He said I needed to relax."

Tara laughed. No, she doubled over laughing, which had Marley running from the kitchen with some blond baby doll tucked beneath her arm.

"What's so funny?" Marley asked, her wide eyes bouncing between her mother and Kate.

"Oh, just something Kate said, honey." Tara swiped beneath her eyes and attempted to control her laughter. "So he told you to relax, which I'm sure you immediately did. And then he watched your planner turn to ash?"

Kate crossed her arms. "Pretty much."

"And he's still breathing?"

"Barely," Kate replied. "He owes me a new planner and don't think I'm not going to pick out the most expensive, thickest one I can find. It will have quotes on every page and a gold-embossed font, and I may just have him spring for the twenty-four-month one instead of the twelve."

Uninterested in the grown-ups' conversation, Marley started skipping around the room with her baby in the air.

"Oh, hitting him in his wallet." Tara feigned a shudder. "That will teach him never to mess with your schedules."

Kate dropped her arms to her sides and rolled her shoulders. "I don't know why the closest people in my life mock my work," she joked. "I mean, I make a killer living off organizing lives. I could help with yours if you'd let me."

Tara held up her hands. "I already let you into my closet. I'm still afraid to mess up those white shirts hanging next to the gray for fear you've set some alarm in there and you'll know if I get them out of order."

Kate laughed as she went to the food table on the back wall. "I'm not that bad," she called over her shoulder. "Besides, your closet was a disaster."

After Sam had left, Tara had needed something to occupy her time, and she'd had Kate and Lucy come over for a girls' night. One thing turned into another and the next thing Kate knew, she was knee-deep in a three-day project to revamp her friend's closet.

"I'm still upset you tossed my favorite sweatshirt," Tara griped, coming to lean against the wall by the table.

Kate rolled her eyes as she straightened up the plastic cups next to the lemonade and sweet tea. "That sweatshirt needed a proper burial and I just helped things along."

"It was a classic."

"No, it was from the junior high volleyball camp we went to and it was hideous."

"Still fit," Tara muttered.

Kate patted her friend's arm. "And that's why I threw it away and secretly hate you. You have never gained an ounce of fat other than when you were pregnant."

Tara quirked a brow. "High metabolism and good gene pool?"

"Still, I can hate you." Kate stepped back and glanced around. "I think we're good to go."

The meeting was due to start in fifteen minutes, which meant people should be rolling in anytime. They always had their regulars, accounting for about eight people. Randomly others would filter in. Some stayed only a few sessions. Some they never saw again.

Ironically, this uplifting support group was how Lucy and Noah met. They would've eventually met at work since he was an officer and Lucy had been a dispatcher. But, as fate would have it, Noah had slipped into the back of the meeting one day and Lucy had made a beeline for him when he tried to sneak out. Noah had lost his wife before coming to Stonerock and Lucy had lost her husband in the war a few years ago. If nothing else came from Helping Hands, at least Lucy and Noah had found true love and a second chance at happiness.

Kate wished that Tara and Sam could do the same, but things weren't looking good. Marley skipped back into the room and ran up to her mom. Tara picked her daughter up and squeezed her tight.

Something flipped in Kate's chest. She wanted a family, a husband to share her life with. But she'd been too busy with her career, a failed engagement and the launch of Helping Hands to make it happen.

An image of Gray flashed through her mind.

No. That was not the direction she needed to take her thoughts. Gray wasn't the marrying type. His father had pressured him over the past few years to settle down, but obviously that wasn't something Gray wanted.

And she needed to remember that he was her everything. She couldn't allow herself to hope for more with him. No, when she married and settled down it wouldn't be with a hunky bar owner with a naughty side and a sleeve of tattoos.

Chapter Ten

Gray finished pulling the wood chairs off the tabletops. He still needed to complete the invoice for next week's beer order and return a call to a new vendor before they opened in two hours.

Owning a bar wasn't just mixing drinks and writing paychecks. There was so much more that went into it, but he'd done it so long—hell, he'd grown up here—he pretty much did everything on autopilot.

Is that how he wanted to spend the rest of his life? Doing the same thing day in and day out? How could a thirty-one-year-old man not have a clue what he wanted to do with his life?

The tempting business proposal from the random

stranger still weighed heavily on him and kept him awake at night.

Granted, the looming deadline wasn't the only thing keeping him awake. A raven-haired vixen posing as his best friend had him questioning everything he'd ever thought to be a truth.

Gray set the last chair on the floor and turned to head toward his office. The old black-and-white picture hanging behind the bar stopped him. He'd seen that picture countless times, passed it constantly, but the image of his grandfather standing in his army uniform outside the bar on the day he bought it seemed to hit home this time.

The back door opened and slammed shut. Only a handful of people used the back door. A sliver of hope hit him as he stared at the doorway to the hall, thinking he'd see Kate step through.

But when his father rounded the corner, Gray smiled, hating how disappointment over not seeing Kate had been his first reaction.

She'd retreated again after their trip. Her pattern shouldn't surprise him, but it did. Whatever she was afraid of, he could battle it. Seriously. Did she not think all of this was freaking him out a little, as well? But there was no way in hell he was just going to ignore this pull toward her. He knew without a doubt that she was being pulled just as fiercely.

"Want a beer?" Gray asked as he circled the bar.

Reece Gallagher went to the opposite side of the

bar and took a seat on one of the stools. "You know what I like."

Gray smiled as he reached for a frosted mug and flipped the tap of his father's favorite brew. He tipped the mug enough to keep the head of the beer just right. Another thing he simply did without thinking.

He'd been meaning to call his dad, but now that he was here, there was no better time to discuss the future of Gallagher's.

Gray set the beer in front of his dad, the frothy top spilling over. He pulled a rag from below the counter and swiped up the moisture.

"Had a visitor the other day," he told his dad.

"Oh, yeah?" Reece took a hearty drink of his beer before setting the mug back on the bar. "Something tells me there's more to the story."

"He offered me more money than I'd know what to do with if I sell him this bar."

His father's dark eyes instantly met his. "Sell Gallagher's? I hope you told him where he could stick his money. Who the hell was this guy?"

Gray swallowed, resting his palms on the smooth bar top. "Businessman from Knoxville. He left me his card and told me I had a month to think about it."

His dad's silver brows drew in as he shifted on his stool and seemed as if he was about ready to come over the bar. "What's there to think about, son?"

Gray figured his father would have this reaction. The bar had been in their family for years and selling had never been an option. Hell, Gray had never thought about selling the place until he'd been presented with the option.

He had to be honest with his dad. There was no reason to gloss this over and pretend everything was fine and he wasn't contemplating the change.

"Maybe I'm not meant to run this bar."

Silence settled between them as the words hung in the air. Gray didn't back down. If his father and the military taught him one thing, it was to never back down from what you believed in.

"You're actually considering this."

Gray nodded even though his father hadn't actually asked. "Something is missing in my life," he said.

His father's response was another pull of his beer. Gray figured he should just lay it all out there. His dad might not like the direction of Gray's thoughts, but he did appreciate and expect honesty.

"I'm thankful for this, all of it. I know you and Grandpa worked hard." He pulled in a deep breath. "I'm just not sure this is what I was meant to do in life."

Reece Gallagher tapped the side of his mug. Whatever was rolling around in his mind, Gray knew his father was formulating a plan to convince him to stay.

"How much were you offered?" his dad finally asked.

Gray threw out the number which resulted in a long, slow whistle from his father.

"That's a hell of a number," he agreed. "And you think this money will ultimately buy you what you want in life? Which is what, exactly?"

Gray shrugged. "I have no clue. There's a void, though. I haven't been able to put my finger on it."

"A wife? Kids?" his dad suggested. "Settling down is a logical step."

Gray pushed off the bar. He was going to need a beer of his own if this was the path the conversation was going to head down.

"I'm not looking for a wife, let alone children."

He pulled a bottle from the cooler behind the bar. Quickly he popped the top and tossed it into the trash.

"I know that's what worked for you and Grandpa," he went on, resting his bottle on the bar. "But I'm not you or him. I'm my own person, and is it so bad that I'm not sure what I want?"

"No," his father agreed. "But I also don't want you making decisions based on money alone, and I certainly don't want you letting all of this go only to find that what you were looking for was here all along."

What the hell did that mean? Stonerock was a great town, but it wasn't necessarily where he wanted to spend his future.

"The decision is ultimately up to you," he dad went on. "You have to understand that I'm not giving you my blessing if you choose to sell. What does he want to do with the bar, anyway?"

Gray took a drink of his beer, then leaned onto his

elbows. "He and his business partner want to make Stonerock like a mini-Nashville. I guess they're looking to buy more businesses in the area and revamp them to draw more tourists."

Reece wrinkled his nose. "That's absurd. Stonerock is just fine the way it is."

Gray finished his beer and tossed his bottle. Then he grabbed his dad's empty mug and set it in the sink below the bar.

"I won't contact him without talking to you first," Gray assured his dad. "I don't want you to think that your opinion doesn't matter or that I'm only looking at dollar signs."

His dad came to his feet and tapped his fingertips on the bar. "I know money can sound good, especially that much, but family is everything, Gray. At the end of the day you only have a few friends and your family that you can count on. Money is just paper."

Why did his dad have to make him feel guilty? Why did he have to add more doubts in his head when he was so close to making a decision?

Reece headed for the back hallway.

"Wait a second," Gray called out. "What did you stop by for to begin with?"

Tossing a glance over his shoulder, his father shook his head. "It's not important."

His footsteps echoed down the hall until they disappeared behind the closing door. Gray stared out at the empty bar, knowing that in just over an hour it would be bustling. That was definitely the main perk to this place. He'd never had to worry about patrons or making money. Gallagher's was the only bar in town and it was a nice place to hang. He was proud of that accomplishment, of the tradition he carried on here.

Emotions filled his throat and squeezed his chest. No matter the decision he made, he'd always wonder if he'd made the right one. If he left, he'd look back and wonder if his father thought him a disappointment. If he stayed, he'd always be looking for something to fill the void. Could he achieve what his heart desired?

Gray wasn't going to be making any decisions tonight. Between the bar and Kate, he wasn't sure how the hell he was supposed to maintain his sanity.

"I have to go," Kate said around a yawn. "I have to meet a client early in the morning to discuss reorganizing her basement for a play-work area."

Lucy put a hand on Kate's arm. "Don't go. I haven't even gotten to the part about the hammock."

Tara busted out laughing and Kate groaned. "Seriously, Lucy. Keep the honeymoon stories to yourself. You came back just as pale as when you left so I know what you were doing."

Lucy shrugged. "But the hammock story is hilarious. Can you even imagine how difficult—"

Kate held up her hands. "I'm getting the visual."

Lucy had been back from her honeymoon only a

day, but they'd been in need of some long overdue girl time. The wedding planning and showers and anticipation had filled their schedules over the past several months.

Tara had invited them over to her house and opened a bottle of wine, and they'd proceeded to just decompress and gossip. Sweet Marley had gone to bed an hour ago, leaving the women to some much-needed adult conversation that wasn't centered around dresses, registries and invitations.

Kate didn't partake in the wine, though. The last time she drank, the *only* time she'd drunk, had changed her entire life, and she was still reeling from the results. Maybe this would just her new normal and she'd have to get used to these unfamiliar emotions that seemed to have taken up residence in her heart.

"Will you hang a bit longer if I promise to hold off on describing the hammock incident?" Lucy asked as she refilled her own wineglass.

Kate shook her head. "I've seriously got so much to do."

"Did you tell Lucy about the planner and the campfire?"

Kate shot a glare at Tara, who sat across on the opposite sofa. The smirk on her friend's face was not funny. Not funny at all.

"A fire and your planner?" Lucy gasped. "I have to hear this. I swear, tell me this and I won't bring up the hammock again."

Kate realized she wasn't going anywhere anytime soon. She sank back into her corner of the couch and replayed her camping story—minus the sex and lustful glances—to her best friends.

"Wait." Lucy held up her hands. "You went camping? That's almost as shocking as the fact Gray burned your planner."

"He forced my hand on the camping thing," she stated. "Well, he didn't force me. Camping was on my life list and he just showed up unannounced—"

"Hold up," Lucy said, incredulous. "What's this life list? Good grief. A girl gets married, has awkward sex in a hammock and misses so much that has happened. Start at the beginning."

"No hammock talk," Kate reminded her.

Lucy shrugged. "Minor slip."

Tara refilled her glass, then propped her bare feet on the couch. "Yes. The beginning of this camping adventure, please."

Kate rolled her eyes. "You already know everything."

"Still makes for a good bedtime story." Tara shrugged. "Besides, I think something is brewing between you and Gray."

"Nothing is brewing. You know we drive each other insane on a good day."

Kate was quick to Δdefend herself, but she and Gray were friends. No, really. No more sex. Just the one time…times two.

"I made a list," Kate started. "I guess you could

call it a bucket list. With turning thirty, I started getting a little anxiety about inching closer to the age my mom was when she died. I figured I better start doing some of the things I really want to try. You just never know how much time you have left."

"Camping made your list?" Lucy asked. "I'm intrigued by what else you've put on there."

Kate slipped off her sandals and pulled her feet back under her. She didn't want to get into the full details of her wishes because…well, she felt that was something she and Gray shared. As strange as that sounded, she'd originally wanted to keep it all to herself, but since he knew, Kate wanted to keep things just between them.

The secrets between her and Gray were mounting up.

"I tried to think of things I'd never done, so, yeah. Camping ranked high," Kate explained. "Once we got settled in and took a hike, I could tell something was bothering Gray. He finally opened up and dropped a bomb on me that someone wants to buy his bar."

"What?" Lucy and Tara both asked.

Kate met her friends' wide eyes and dropped jaws with a nod. "He said some guy came in and offered him an insane amount of money to purchase Gallagher's. Said something about buying properties around the town to update them and make them more city-like."

"Our town doesn't need updating," Lucy stated.

"The reason people live here is because they like the small-town atmosphere. If they wanted a city feel, they'd move there. I wonder if Drake is aware of this. Surely these guys had the decency to talk to our mayor."

Kate shrugged. "Just telling you what I know."

Tara set her wineglass on the coffee table and shifted to face Kate. "Is Gray seriously considering giving up the bar?"

"He hasn't turned the offer down."

Which honestly surprised her. He'd explained the whole thing about feeling something missing in his life, but at the same time, this was his family's legacy. A piece of history that had just been handed to him. Did he even realize how lucky he was? She'd give anything to have a piece of her parents handed down to her, some way to still hold on to them.

Which was why tracing her family genealogy had made her list.

"Wow." Lucy took another sip of her wine. "When will he decide what he's doing?"

"The guy gave him a deadline. Next week sometime." Kate stretched her legs out and felt around for her shoes. She really did need to get going. Not just because of the work thing. She didn't want to get back into the camping conversation and Tara's speculation that something was up. "He's going to talk to his dad and feel him out, though I imagine that won't go very well."

No doubt he'd let her know exactly how that talk

went. Then he'd probably call her out on dodging him since they'd returned from their trip. She hadn't been dodging him, exactly. She'd been working and she assumed he had, as well.

Besides, she just needed a break after those two days together. The man consumed her every thought lately and when they were together he was…well, even more irresistible and in her face.

What did all of this mean? How could she let her Gray go from being her best friend to lover, then try to put him back in the best friend zone? It shouldn't be that difficult to keep him locked away in that particular section of her heart. Isn't that what she did for a living? Put everything in a neat and tidy order?

So why the hell couldn't she do that with her personal life?

Kate finally said her goodbyes to her best girlfriends and agreed to meet them at Ladies' Night on Wednesday. She hadn't been for a while and was overdue—something Gray had noticed and called her out on. And, well, she could use a night of dancing and just having a good time.

That would prove to Gray that she wasn't dodging him…right?

Kate headed home, her mind working through all she needed to get done over the next couple of days. She was still in need of a good personal planner. She had looked at a few, but hadn't made a commitment yet. Whatever she chose, Gray would feel it in his wallet. That would teach him not to mess with her things anymore.

As she pulled into her drive, she noticed a sporty black car parked on the street directly in front of her house. Her eyes darted to the porch, where a man in a suit sat on one of her white rockers.

Kate barely took her eyes off him as she put the car in Park and killed the engine. Of all people to make an unexpected visit, her cheating, lying ex was the last man she ever expected to see again.

Chapter Eleven

Gripping her purse, Kate headed up her stone walkway. "What are you doing here, Chris?"

Always clean-cut and polished, Chris Percell came to his feet and shoved his hands in his pockets.

Who wore a suit at this time of night? And in this humidity? Not that his wardrobe was a concern of hers. No, the main issues here were that he stood on her porch without an invitation and she hadn't heard a word from him in years. Granted, once he'd left, she hadn't wanted to hear a word from the cheating bastard.

Kate didn't mount the steps. He had about three seconds to state his business and then she was going in her house and locking the door. She hadn't been lying when she told her friends she was tired and still had some work to do, so this unexpected visitor was not putting her in the best of moods.

"You look good, Kate."

Chris started down the steps toward her. Now she did dodge him and go on up to her porch. When she turned, he stood on the bottom step, smiling up at her.

"It's been a long time," he stated.

"Not long enough. What do you want?"

With a shrug, he crossed his arms and shifted his stance. "I was hoping we could talk."

"Most people just text." She'd deleted him from her phone long ago, but still. Showing up unannounced was flat-out rude. Not that he had many morals or even common decency.

"I wasn't sure if you'd respond."

"I wouldn't," she told him.

He propped one foot on the next step and smoothed a hand over his perfectly parted hair. "After all these years, you're still angry?"

She didn't know whether to laugh at his stupidity or throw her purse at him and pray she hit him in the head hard enough to knock some damn sense into him.

No purse should be treated that way, so she adjusted the strap on her shoulder and held it tight.

"Angry?" she asked with a slight laugh. "I'd have to feel something to actually be angry with you."

"Kate." Chris lowered his tone as if to appeal to

her good side. She no longer had one where he was concerned. "Could I come in for a bit just to talk?"

"No. And actually, it's a bit creepy that you're on my porch waiting on me to get home."

"I haven't been here long," he assured her. "Maybe I should come back tomorrow. Can I take you for coffee?"

Kate stared down at the clean-cut man who probably still got bimonthly manicures. She couldn't help but wonder what in the hell she'd ever seen in him to begin with. Coffee with a man wearing a suit? She'd prefer champagne served up by a sexy tattooed-up bar owner.

Oh, no.

No, no, no.

Now was not the time to discover that her feelings were sliding into more than just friendship with Gray. Chris continued to stare at her, waiting for her answer, but she was having a minor mental breakdown.

"I'm busy tomorrow," she finally replied. "Good night, Chris."

Without waiting for him to respond, Kate pulled her key from her purse and quickly let herself into the house. She flicked the dead bolt back into place and smacked the porch lights off.

What on earth had flashed through her mind when Chris mentioned taking her for coffee? She loved coffee and Stonerock had the best little coffee house on the edge of town. Not that she would even entertain the thought of having coffee with that slime bag.

But Gray?

Everything in her thought process lately circled back to that man. Her planner, her bucket list, her drinks, her most satisfying sexual experiences.

Kate groaned as she made her way toward her bedroom. What she needed to do was spend more time with Tara and Lucy. So much one-on-one with Gray had obviously clouded her judgment and left her confused and mixing amazing sex with feelings that shouldn't be developing.

But Tara was busy with her own life and Lucy was still in that newlywed bliss phase. Ladies' Night would definitely be her best bet to get back to where she needed to be mentally. Letting lose, being carefree, and not worrying about anything would surely cleanse her mind of all lustful thoughts of her best friend.

Sex really did cloud the mind. And great sex… well, maybe she just needed sleep. If she weren't so exhausted, perhaps Gray wouldn't have filled her mind the second Chris started talking about taking her out.

Gray hadn't even taken her out. They weren't in any way dating. They were going on about their way like always—just adding in a few toe-curling orgasms along the way.

Kate pushed aside all thoughts of Chris showing up, Gray and his ability to make her want more than she should and the fact he may be selling his bar and leaving. She couldn't get wrapped up in lives and circumstances she had no control over. As much as she thrived on micromanaging, realistically, she had to let go.

After pulling on her favorite sleep shirt, Kate slid beneath her sheets and adjusted her pillows against the upholstered headboard. She unplugged her iPad from the nightstand and pulled up her schedule for the following day. Yes, her schedule was in both paper and e-format.

After glancing over her schedule, she went to her personal blog. So many blogs failed, but Kate prided herself on being a marketing genius. She honed in on her niche market, taking full advantage of social media platforms that drove her clients to her site, thus turning them into paying customers.

Not many people could do their dream job and work from home. Kate knew how blessed and lucky she was to have such a fabulous life.

Though seeing Lucy so happy with love and Tara with sweet Marley made Kate wonder if she was missing out.

Tara clicked on the tab to bring up her bucket list. At the bottom she added the word "family" in bold font. Ultimately that would be her main goal once she'd achieved the others. She wasn't going to rush it, she wanted to wait on the right man to come along. She was definitely ready to take that step toward a broader future.

Stifling a yawn, Kate placed her device back on her nightstand and clicked the light off. As she fluffed her pillows and rolled over, she hoped she would fall asleep right away and not dream of the sexy bar owner who had occupied her thoughts every night.

But she found herself smiling. She couldn't help herself. There was no greater man in her life, and even though things were a little unbalanced right now, she fully intended on keeping him at an arm's length. For real this time.

"Thanks, darlin', but I'm busy tonight."

Ladies' Night always brought in the flirtatious women with short skirts and plunging necklines. Being single didn't hurt business, either, but he'd never picked up a woman in his bar. That wasn't good business and certainly not a reputation he wanted hovering over his establishment.

Gray extracted himself from the clutches of the blonde at the table in the corner. That's what he got for coming out from behind his post. His staff had been busy so he'd taken the table their drinks.

Back behind the safety of the bar, Gray tapped on the computer and started filling more drink orders. Jacob ran the finger foods from the kitchen. The menu remained small and simple but enough to keep people thirsty, because the drinks were by far the moneymaker.

The DJ switched the song to one that seriously

made Gray's teeth itch. "It's Raining Men" blared through the hidden surround sound speakers. Considering the crowd and the cheers and squeals, Gray was definitely in the minority here.

One night. He could live through terrible music for one night a week. Wednesday nights brought in the most revenue. Women from all walks of life came out in droves. Some were celebrating bachelorette parties. Some were stay-at-home moms who needed a break. Sometimes a group of employees got together to decompress after work. Whatever their situation was, Gray—and his bottom line—was thrilled he'd decided to add this night when he'd taken over.

As he placed three margaritas on the bar for one of his staff to take to table eleven, he glanced at the front door when it opened.

Finally.

Gray didn't even care that his heart skipped a little at the sight of Kate. He was done ignoring the way he felt when she was near. He just…damn it, he wanted her to stop avoiding him. He needed her stability, the security she brought to their friendship.

He hadn't spoken with her since he'd talked to his dad. Just the thought of that conversation had him questioning what to do. Clearly his father would be heartbroken over losing Gallagher's, but Gray just kept thinking back to how free he would be if he was able to explore his own interests.

His eyes drifted back to Kate. She'd settled in a booth with Tara and Lucy. When her gaze landed on him, she might as well have touched him with her bare hands. Immediate heat spread through him, and the second she flashed that radiant smile, Gray nearly toppled the glass he'd been holding.

After returning her smile, he returned his focus to the orders. No woman had ever made him falter on the job before. Then again, no woman was Kate McCoy.

As he worked on filling orders, he randomly glanced her way. He knew exactly which drinks were going to that table. Those three were so predictable. Tara always wanted a cosmo, Lucy stuck with a light beer and Kate went with soda.

It wasn't long before another song blared through the speakers that had Gray cringing, but the dance floor instantly filled with women. Kate and her friends were right in the midst of the action.

That little dress she wore had his gut tightening. The loose hem slid all over her thighs as she wiggled that sweet body on the dance floor. She'd piled her hair up on top of her head, but the longer she danced, the more stray strands fell around her face, her neck.

Get a grip

"Hey, baby. You ever take time for a dance?"

Gray flashed a smile to the redhead leaning over the bar at just the right angle to give him a complete visual of her cleavage and bra of choice.

"Who would make all these drinks if I went dancing?" he yelled over the music.

She reached across the bar and ran her fingertip down his chest. "I think if you got on that dance floor, we'd all forget about our drinks. At least for a little while."

Someone slammed a glass next to him, jerking Gray's attention from the flirtatious patron.

He turned just in time to see Kate walking away, her empty glass on the bar.

"Looks like you made someone's drink wrong," the redhead stated, lowering her lids. "You can make me anything you want."

Gray stepped back, causing her hand to fall from his chest. "Where are you and your friends sitting?" he asked. "I'll send over a pitcher of margaritas."

Her smile widened as she gestured to their table. Apparently the idea of free booze was more appealing than him…which was perfectly fine. Right now, he was more intrigued with the way Kate had acted. She'd slammed that glass pretty close to his arm on purpose and then walked away without a word.

Jealous?

Gray couldn't help but smile as he got the pitcher ready. If Kate was jealous, then maybe she was ready to see where this new level of friendship would take them. Perhaps she'd missed him in the days they'd been apart and she'd thought more about their time in the mountains.

Maybe she'd finally realized how good they were together and that it was silly to put restrictions on their intimacy. He spotted her back out on the dance floor talking to Lucy. Lucy nodded in response to whatever she said and Kate walked away.

Gray picked up empty glasses and wiped off the bar where a few ladies had just sat, all the while keeping his gaze on Kate. She went back to the booth and grabbed her purse.

Well, hell. She was pissed and leaving? All because some woman flirted with him?

If she was that upset, then she was definitely jealous. Gray had every intention of playing right into that little nugget of information.

Gray lost track of Kate, but he never saw the front door open, which meant she had to be inside somewhere. He glanced at his watch and realized they still had another two business hours to go. He couldn't get to Kate for a while, but she better be ready for him, because he wasn't backing down from this fight. He was damn well going to call her out on her jealousy and forbid her to make any excuses for why they shouldn't be together.

Gray couldn't wait to get her alone again.

Chapter Twelve

This was the most ridiculous thing she'd ever done in her entire life. But hey, at least she could mark spontaneity off her life list.

Kate stared at the clock on Gray's nightstand. The bar had closed thirty minutes ago. She knew he had cleanup down to a science and he should be wrapping things up any minute.

She thought coming up here to cool off would help. Seeing that trampy redhead raking her false nail down Gray's chest had set something off inside Kate she didn't want to label…because it smacked her right in the face with jealousy.

Why was she jealous? Kate knew full well that women found Gray sexy and did nearly anything to get his attention. But things were different now. Yes, they were just friends, but everything had changed.

What would he say when he came up here and found her in his bed? Would he tell her they'd agreed to call it quits after the camping? Would he climb in bed and give her another night to remember?

Kate came to her feet and grabbed the dress she'd flung at the bottom of the bed. This was a mistake. She looked like an utter fool. No, a desperate fool, and she needed to get the hell out of here before Gray came in.

The front door to his apartment clicked shut, followed by the dead bolt. Too late to run.

She clutched the dress to her chest, feeling even more ridiculous now. Why had she put that damn "be more spontaneous" idea on her list? And why had she let that busty tramp bring out the green-eyed monster?

Heavy footsteps sounded down the hall seconds before Gray filled the doorway. His dark eyes widened as they raked over her. There was no way she could move. Just that simple, visual lick he gave her had her rooted in place.

His eyes snapped back up to hers. "Put the dress down."

Kate dropped it at her feet before thinking twice. That low command gave her little choice but to obey. Warmth spread through her. There was no denying exactly why she'd come up here, just as there was no denying that heated look in his eyes.

"You came up here a while ago." He leaned one broad shoulder against the door frame and continued to rake his eyes across her body. "What have you been doing?"

"Second-guessing myself," she murmured.

Gray's lips twitched. "Is that so? I don't recall sneaking into a man's bedroom on your life list."

"I was trying to check off spontaneity."

"Is that so?"

Kate crossed her arms over her chest. "I'm feeling a little silly standing here like this. Are you just going to stay over there and stare at me?"

"Maybe I'm looking at you because you deserve to be valued."

Oh, no. He couldn't say things like that to her. Statements so bold only pushed them deeper into this …whatever the technical term was. *Friends* seemed too tame of a label considering she stood in his bedroom wearing only her underwear.

"Chris showed up at my house."

Why did she blurt that out? She prided herself on planning everything, even her words. But somehow hearing him mention her being valued made her think of the jerk who thought the opposite.

Gray stood straight up and took a step toward her. "What the hell did he want?"

Kate laughed. "To talk. He invited me to coffee."

The muscle in his jaw clenched. "Did you go?" he all but growled.

"No. I demanded he leave and I haven't heard from him since."

Gray's eyes narrowed. "He's trying to get you back."

"After all this time and after what he did? He's a fool."

"Tell me if he comes back."

Kate stared up into those dark eyes. "You're jealous."

Gray slid his palms up her bare arms, over her shoulders, and hooked his thumbs in her bra straps. "Like you were jealous downstairs?"

Tipping her chin up, she met his mocking stare. "I was not jealous."

Gray's fingertips left the straps and slid over the swell of her breasts. Tingles raced through her body.

"You cracked the glass you slammed down." One finger slid between her breasts and back up. "Seemed like you were upset about something."

"Consider the glass payment for the panties you ripped off me."

If possible, his eyes darkened at the mention of her underwear. In one swift move, he flicked the front closure of her bra and had it off. When he gripped the edge of her panties and met her eyes, she smiled.

"You going for two?" she asked, quirking a brow.

He gave a yank, and the sound of ripping material answered her question. Suddenly she stood before him completely naked and in the bright light of his bedroom while he was completely clothed.

"This is hardly fair," she informed him.

"You snuck up to my apartment and came to my bed," he reminded her. "You're playing by my rules now, Kate."

How did the man continually get sexier? Seriously. Looks were one thing, but the way he treated her, spoke to her...how would she feel when this came to an end?

"I wasn't going to do this again," she muttered, mostly to herself.

"And I wasn't going to let you run, either." He banded an arm around her waist and jerked her body against his. "Why is there a time limit on what we're doing? We both like it. Neither one of us is dating anyone. It makes sense."

Kate closed her eyes. "Because we could lose ourselves and forget who we really are."

He leaned down and nipped her lips. "Maybe we're only just discovering who we really are."

Those words barely registered before he lifted her off her feet and carried her to his bed. He eased her down onto the plain gray sheets that were still rumpled from when he'd gotten out of them. She'd never been in his bedroom. They'd been friends forever, but crossing this threshold was taking things to a whole new territory.

Gray eased back, leaving her lying spread out. She watched as he reached behind his neck and jerked the black tee up and over his head. After he tossed it into the corner, he started unfastening his jeans, all while keeping those heavy-lidded eyes on her.

"You look good here, Kate."

She closed her eyes. Maybe if she didn't look at him when he said such meaningful words, they wouldn't penetrate her soul. But he kept saying little things. No, not little, not in the terms of the impact they had.

Instead of responding, because she truly had no words, she lifted her knees to make room for him. Once he'd gotten protection from his nightstand, she reached out, taking him in her arms. His weight pressed her further into the bed. She wasn't sure how she looked here, but she knew she liked it. Being wrapped up in Gray and knowing they shared something no one else knew about…there was a thrill to what they were doing.

A thrill she wasn't sure she ever wanted to see end.

But was he on the same page? If she threw out that she was having stronger feelings, what would he say? Would he tell her they were done with sex? Would he tell her they could be friends and have sex only as long as they were both single? Because suddenly, she wondered if there could be more.

"Hey."

Kate focused on the man who flanked her head with his forearms and smoothed her hair away from her face.

"Stay with me," he murmured.

Curling her fingers around his bare shoulders, Kate smiled. "I wouldn't be anywhere else."

Gray joined their bodies and Kate locked her ankles behind his back. She wanted to stay just like this, to forget the outside world, to ignore any warning that went off in her head about what could go wrong. Because right now, everything in her world was absolutely perfect.

Gray's lips slid over her skin, along her jawline, down her neck, along her chest. Kate arched into him, needing more and silently begging him to give it to her. Gray murmured something into her ear and she couldn't make it out. He'd done that before and she wondered what he was saying, but that was something she'd ask later. She'd rather enjoy the euphoria and sweet bliss of being in his arms...in his bed.

In a move that shocked her, Gray held on to her and flipped them until he was on his back and she straddled him. The way he looked up at her...

A girl could get used to a man looking at her like she was the only good thing in his world.

Gray gripped her hips and Kate's body instantly responded to his strength. His fingers bit into her as she flattened her palms on his chest and let the moment completely consume her.

Before Kate's body ceased trembling, Gray's stilled beneath her. His lips thinned. His head tipped back. His eyes shut. But his grip on her never lightened. She remained where she was, watching the play of emotions across his face.

Slowly he relaxed beneath her. As he slid his hands up over the dip in her waist and urged her down, Kate smiled. She fell against his chest and closed her eyes.

"What now?" she asked, unable to stop herself.

His chest vibrated with the soft rumble of laughter. "We don't need to plan the next move. Relax."

When she started to set up, he flattened his hand on her back. "You can stay just like this a few more minutes."

She could, but she had questions. So many questions and only he could answer them. Well, they could figure them out together, but what was going to happen when she told him she might want more? He'd never even acted like he wanted a relationship. They had sex. They had never even been on a real date.

Kate couldn't take it anymore. She sat up and shifted off him. With her back to Gray, she sat on the edge of the bed and leaned down to pick up her discarded dress.

"We really need to talk."

Silence filled the air, as she'd expected it would once she uttered those five words that would put any man's hackles up.

Kate threw a glance over her shoulder. Gray lay there naked as you please, with his arms folded behind his head. His eyes held hers, but he still said nothing even when she raised a brow, silently begging him to speak.

"Why are you making this difficult?" she asked.

She came to her feet and threw her dress on, sans all undergarments. When she spun around toward the bed and crossed her arms over her chest, Gray merely smiled. Still naked, still fully in charge of this situation, because he just watched her. The man could be utterly infuriating.

"What are we doing?" she muttered, shaking her head. "Seriously? Are we going to keep doing this? Is there more?"

Her heart beat so fast, she wondered if he could see the pulse in her neck. Again without a word, Gray came to his feet and strutted from the room.

She threw her arms out. "Well, that went well," she whispered to the empty room.

Moments later, he came back in, still not the least bit concerned with his state of undress. He carried two wine stems between his fingers and in the other hand he had a champagne bottle.

"This is another bottle of what you had the other night." He set everything on the nightstand and poured her a glass. "You need another drink if we're going to get into this discussion."

"Drinking isn't the answer," she retorted.

He picked up the glass and handed it to her. "I never said it was. But I brought this bottle up earlier and got sidetracked when I found you naked in my room."

She took the glass but didn't take a sip yet. "Why

did you bring it to begin with? I didn't take you for a champagne drinker."

"I'm not, but I knew you were up here so I brought it for you."

Kate jerked. "How did you know I came up here? I was discreet."

Gray laughed as he filled his own glass and then downed it in one gulp. He set the glass back on the nightstand and turned toward her.

"I'm a pretty smart guy, Kate." He pointed toward her glass. "You're going to want to start on that."

She took a small drink, relishing the bubbles that burst in her mouth. Champagne really wasn't bad at all.

"You were jealous," he started, holding up his hand when she opened her mouth to argue. "You were, so be quiet for a minute."

Kate took another drink and sank onto the edge of the bed. "Could you at least put something on? It's hard to concentrate with all that hanging out."

Gray laughed and turned toward his dresser, where a stack of clean laundry lay neatly folded. He grabbed a pair of black boxer briefs and tugged them on.

"Better?"

Actually, no. The briefs hugged his narrow hips, drawing her attention to that perfect V of muscles leading south. Mercy, how had she missed all of his flawless features in the past?

She took another drink.

"So you were jealous," he went on.

"Move to something else," she growled.

Gray laughed, propping his hands on those hips she tried so hard to stop staring at. "Fine. Then I saw you grab your purse and disappear, only the front door didn't open and I couldn't get a clear view of the back hall. Nobody goes that way, but I had a feeling my Kate had done just that."

She narrowed her eyes. "Jacob told you."

"He didn't have to say anything."

Kate polished off her champagne and set her empty glass next to his. When she glanced back up at him, she shivered at the look in his eyes.

"You didn't like that woman flirting with me. That was a good piece of information to have."

Kate hated that she'd let her emotions get the better of her. "Fine. I was jealous."

Gray knelt down in front of her and clasped her hands in his. "I didn't think you'd admit it."

"Why hide it? We may just be having sex, but that doesn't mean I want to see some woman pawing you."

Kate stared down at their joined hands and willed herself to be strong and just say what she wanted to say. But before she could tell him her thoughts, he placed one hand beneath her chin and tipped her face to meet his.

Gray leaned forward and nipped at her lips before murmuring, "Marry me."

Chapter Thirteen

Why wasn't she saying anything?

Gray waited.

"Kate?"

She blinked. "Marry you? But we've never discussed anything like that."

When she came to her feet, her abrupt movement had him standing as well. Then she began to pace his room. She couldn't go far in the small space, but since he had only a bed and dresser, she didn't have much to maneuver around.

"Marry you," she repeated beneath her breath as she turned on her heel to walk in the other direction.

"Why not?" he asked. "We get along, we're good

together in bed, and we just understand each other. That's more than most married couples have."

She stopped and stared at him as if he had grown another nose on the side of his head. "Why on earth do you want to marry me?"

"I talked to Dad about selling the bar." Now it was his turn to pace because the thought of everything closing in on him made him twitchy. "He's most definitely not on board and he seems to think I just need to settle down. Perhaps this way, I could sell it and you and I could use that money to start over somewhere. Or hell, build a house here. Whatever. We'd have freedom and that's all that matters."

He'd come to stand directly in front of her, but she continued to stare. No, glare would best describe what she was doing now. There was something he couldn't quite pinpoint in her eyes. Gone was the desire he'd seen moments ago.

"So, what, I'm just a means to pacify your dad so you can collect a check?" she asked. With a shake of her head, she let out a humorless laugh. "I was already going to marry one jerk who obviously didn't get me. It's quite clear you never understood me either if you think I'll marry you."

Anger simmered within him, but he didn't want to lash out.

"What the hell is wrong with marrying me?" he asked.

"I want to know your first thought when I asked why you wanted to marry me. Don't think about what I want to hear. Just tell me the first thing that comes into your head."

This was a trap. Somewhere in that statement she'd set a trap for him and he was about to fall headfirst into it.

"I think it makes sense," he answered honestly. "What's there to think about?"

She stared at him a bit longer and that's when he saw it. Hurt. That emotion he couldn't pin down before had been pain and it stared back at him plain as day. He'd seen that look before from patrons who wanted to drink their worries away. He'd seen it too often. But he was completely baffled by why the hell she stared at him with such anguish.

"What did I say?"

She chewed on her bottom lip for a moment before skirting around him and picking up her underwear and bra. He watched as she dressed fully and then sat on the edge of his bed to pull her sandals on.

"Where are you going?"

Without looking up, she adjusted her shoe and came to her feet. "Home. I've had enough of…whatever this is. We never should've slept together."

He crossed the room and took her shoulders, forcing her to face him. "What the hell are you talking about? Is this because I asked you to marry me?"

Her eyes swam with unshed tears and he wished like hell he knew why she was this upset.

"Do you love me, Gray?"

"What?" Her question stunned him. "Of course

I love you. I've loved you since the seventh grade. What kind of a question is that?"

She blinked, causing a tear to spill down her cheek. He swiped the pad of his thumb over her creamy skin. His heart ached at seeing her hurt, but hell if he knew how to fix this.

"It's a legitimate question, considering you proposed," she said, her voice soft, sad. "This isn't working for me anymore."

Kate shrugged from his arms and stepped back. She tilted her chin and squared her shoulders as if going into warrior mode before his eyes.

"You want freedom?" she asked. "Then go. Take that fat check, sell the bar and just go."

"What the hell are you so angry about?" he asked…well, more like yelled, because damn it, he could not figure her out.

"I never thought you'd use me or consider me plan B for your life." She swatted at another tear that streaked down her cheek. "You're only asking me to marry you to pacify your father. That man would do anything for you and he's all you have left. Do you know how lucky you are? Do you understand that if I had a parent in my life, I'd do anything to make them proud of me?"

Now he was pissed. Gray fisted his hands at his sides and towered over her as he took a step forward. "You think my father isn't proud of me? Of what I've done here? You know I'm sorry about your parents, but damn it, Kate, you can't always throw that in my face."

She recoiled as if he'd hit her. Gray muttered a string of curses beneath his breath as he raked a hand through his hair.

"That's not what I meant," he said.

She held up her hands. "You said exactly what you meant. We don't see eye to eye on things anymore. Just another reason why I need to go and this…all of it has to stop."

His heart clenched. "What do you mean, 'all of it'?"

"I knew we couldn't keep our friendship and sex separate," she cried. Tears streamed down her cheeks and she didn't even bother swiping them away. "Then you throw out an engagement like it's a simple fix to your problems. Did you ever think that maybe I'd want to marry someone who actually loves me? That I don't just want to settle?"

"I said I loved you," he practically shouted. "What more do you want?"

The brief smile that flashed amid the tears nearly gutted him. Pain radiated from her and if he knew what he'd done to crush her, he'd fix it.

"You don't mean it," she whispered. "Not in the way I need you to."

A rumble of thunder and a quick flash of lightning interrupted the tense moment. Within seconds, rain pelted the windows. Kate stared at him another second before she turned away and headed toward the door. Gray had a sinking feeling that if she walked out that door, she might never come back…not even as his friend.

"Don't go, Kate. Not like this."

She stilled, but didn't face him.

"We can work this out."

"I think we've said enough," she replied.

He took a step toward her, but didn't reach for her like he desperately wanted to. "At least let me drive you home. You're upset and it's starting to storm."

Those bright blue eyes shining with tears peered over her shoulder. "I'd rather take my chances with the storm outside than the one surrounding us."

And then she was gone.

Gray stared at the spot where she'd just stood, then he glanced to the empty glasses, the rumpled sheets.

What the hell had just happened here?

Well, there was the proposal that had taken them both by surprise. But in his defense, the moment the words were out of his mouth, he hadn't regretted them.

He did love her. They'd been friends forever, so what kind of question was that? And what did she mean by saying he didn't love her the way she needed him to? He'd always been there for her, hadn't he?

Gray turned from the bedroom. He couldn't stay in there, not when the sheets smelled like her, not when just the sight of that bed had him recalling how perfect she'd looked lying there.

He stalked down the hall and into the living room. The storm grew closer as the thunder and lightning hit simultaneously. The electricity flickered once, twice, then went out.

Perfect. Pitch black to match his mood.

Gray went to the window and looked down into the parking lot beside the bar. Kate's car still sat there.

Without thinking, he fumbled his way through the dark to throw on a pair of jeans, not bothering with shoes. He raced down the back steps and out the rear entrance.

Instantly he was soaked, but he didn't care. If Kate was still here, she was sitting in her car, upset. He knew that as well as he knew his name.

He tapped on the driver's window. Kate started the car and slid the window down a sliver.

"Get out of the storm," she yelled.

"I will when I know you're all right."

The damn street lights were out so he couldn't see her face, but he saw enough shimmer in her eyes to know she wasn't fine, not at all.

"You're soaked. Go inside, Gray. We're done."

He jerked open her door, propping one arm up on the car, and leaned down to get right in her face. "We're not done, Kate. You can't brush me aside."

The lights from her dash lit up her face. She stared at him for a moment before shaking her head.

"I'm going home. I need some space."

He knew what that was code for. She wanted

to push him away and try to figure everything out herself. Hell no. Yes, he'd upset her, but he wasn't backing down. This was bigger than selling the bar, pleasing his father or some lame marriage proposal.

Kate had legitimately been hurt by their conversation. She'd opened herself and came to his room. He could only imagine the courage that had taken.

"You can have your space," he told her, swiping the rain from his eyes. "But know that you can't keep me away. I'm not going anywhere, Kate."

He didn't give her a chance to reply. Gray gripped the back of her head and covered her mouth with his. Quick, fierce, impossible to forget, that's the kiss he delivered before he stepped back and closed her car door.

The window slid up as she put the car in Drive and pulled out of the lot. He stood in the midst of the storm, watching her taillights disappear into the dark night.

The thunder continued to rumble and a bolt of lightning streaked across the sky. Gray rubbed his chest as he headed back inside. He'd always ached for her when she'd gotten upset. But this was different.

Somehow with that surprise proposal, he'd severed something they shared. He'd tainted their friendship and put a dark cloud over their lives. All he'd wanted to do was make his father happy and somehow that had blown up in his face.

Gray knew sleep wasn't coming anytime soon,

so he started plotting. If the damn electricity would come back on, he could put his plan into motion and maybe salvage some semblance of this friendship.

Chapter Fourteen

Kate clicked Send on her blog and sat back to admire the new layout she'd implemented on her site. Thanks to sleepless nights, she'd had plenty of time to work on cleaning up her pages a bit. She now had everything organized and easier to maneuver.

But she was in no mood to celebrate. For the past two mornings she'd been sick as a dog. She'd also missed her period and there was a home pregnancy test in her bathroom that mocked her every time she went in. There was no need to take it. She knew.

The birth control she'd switched from pill to patch had come during their camping trip, there was no questioning how this happened.

She hadn't heard from Gray in two weeks. The

deadline had passed for him to make a decision on the bar, but he hadn't told her anything. He hadn't texted, hadn't called. He'd warned her he'd give her space and he'd kept his word.

Damn it, why did she have to miss him so much? What was he going to say when she told him about the baby? Most likely he'd take that Neanderthal attitude and try to convince her to marry him.

Kate glanced at the clock. She really needed to get some lunch. The crackers and ginger ale this morning had worn off. Well, they hadn't stayed down, so they'd worn off immediately.

She scrolled through her newly uploaded blog discussing why organization made for a better attitude. People in general were calmer if the world around them was in order so they didn't feel as if they were living in chaos. She'd even added a new buy button to the site, along with a note stating that all first-time clients would receive a 10 percent discount.

Her newsletter was set to go out this evening, so the timing of this post was perfect. Of course, she'd planned it that way.

Kate pushed her chair back and came to her feet. A slight wave of dizziness overcame her. Gripping the edge of her desk, she closed her eyes and waited for it to pass.

What would Lucy and Tara say? They didn't even know she and Gray had been intimate. They would be hurt that she hadn't confided in them, but she just hadn't been ready and then she thought things were going to go back to normal and now…well, this was her new normal.

Kate's cell buzzed and vibrated on her desk top. She sank back into her chair and stared at the screen, not recognizing the number. New clients contacted her all the time, so ignoring the call wasn't an option.

"Hello?"

"Ms. McCoy?"

She didn't recognize the male voice on the other end. "Yes."

"My name is Steven Sanders. I'm with a group out of Nashville called Lost and Found Family."

Intrigued, Kate eased back in her seat and kept her eyes shut. The room had stopped spinning, but she wasn't taking any chances right now.

"What can I do for you, Mr. Sanders?"

"Actually, it's what I can do for you," he countered. "I was given your contact information by Gray Gallagher. He wanted me to talk with you about tracing your family and finding your heritage. Is this a good time to talk?"

So many things swirled around in her mind. Gray had called someone to help her find her family? But he hadn't talked to her or even texted. Why hadn't he told her about this? Why was he being so nice when she'd turned him down and left in the midst of a storm?

"Sure," she replied. "Um…sorry. This is all just a bit of a surprise."

The man chuckled on the other end of the line.

"Gray was adamant I call you as soon as I could, but I was trying to get another case wrapped up before contacting you. He made me vow to give your case special attention."

Something warmed inside her, something that brought tears to her eyes. She leaned forward, resting her elbows on her desk.

"Well, I appreciate that," she replied. "But I understand I'm probably not your only client. What information do you need from me?"

Steven went on to explain the information Gray had already delivered to him. He asked her about her mother's maiden name, her skin color, eye color, hair color. He went through her father's description. Then he asked for birthdays, where they were born and any grandparents' names she might know.

"This gives me a bit to go on to get started," Steven said after about a half hour of gathering information. "Should I call or email you when I have more questions?"

"I'm fine with either," she replied. "I can't thank you enough. I never knew really who to call to get started on this. You can bill me through email and I'll—"

"Oh, no, ma'am. Mr. Gallagher already took care of the bill, and any further charges will be sent to him."

Kate wasn't going to get into an argument with this guy. He had no clue about the whirlwind of emotions that continued to swirl around her and Gray. The poor guy was just doing his job.

"Thanks so much for taking on this case," she replied. "I look forward to hearing from you."

"I'll be in touch."

She disconnected the call and stood back up, thankfully no longer dizzy. As she made her way toward the kitchen, she went over in her mind what she wanted to say to Gray. He'd already helped her by tracking down someone who could research her ancestry. He didn't need to pay for it, too. And he'd done all of this after they'd stopped speaking.

The idea that he'd started working on a portion of her life list had tears burning her eyes. No matter what had transpired between them, he was still determined to be there for her.

Kate made a quick peanut butter sandwich and grabbed a bottle of water and a banana before heading back to her office. There was no dodging Gray anymore. She needed to thank him for hiring the genealogy investigator, plus tell him about the baby.

If she thought their dynamics had been changed before with just sex, this would certainly alter everything they'd ever known. She had to be positive before going to him and she had to know exactly what to say.

Kate would definitely take the test to be sure, but he deserved to know. This was definitely something they needed to work on together.

Looked like she wasn't going to be putting him in

that friend category anymore. She wasn't ready to put him in the husband category, either. He'd honestly hurt her when he'd said why he wanted to marry her.

How could he be so blind? How could he not see that she wanted someone who genuinely loved her? Like *in love* with her?

She'd been on the verge of telling him she was falling for him when he blurted out the proposal, destroying any hope she might have had that their bond could go deeper than friendship. And now she was carrying his child. If this wasn't the most warped situation ever, she didn't know what was.

Ladies' Night was tonight and in their group texts, Lucy and Tara had already been vocal about wanting to go. Kate figured now would be as good a time as any to go out, try to have fun and not freak out about her entire life getting turned upside down.

Because as scared, nervous and anxious as she was about this child—along with a gamut of other emotions—the truth of the matter was…she was happy. She had no family, but she was creating her very own. No, this was definitely not planned and, surprisingly, she was okay

This wasn't a schedule or a job. This was a child. Her child.

Would Gray still want to take the money from the sale of the bar? She couldn't stand the thought of him leaving, but he needed to be aware of just how much their lives were about to change.

Tonight. She'd go tonight and thank him for the

genealogy specialist. Then, once the bar closed, she'd take him upstairs and tell him about the baby.

First, though, she had a test to take.

As Wednesday nights went, the bar was crazier than usual. He'd begged one of his waitresses to come in on her night off. He never begged. He'd even offered her an extra paid day off if she just came in for a few hours to help bartend. Jacob was in the kitchen filling in for the cook, who'd come down with some cold or whatever.

It was just a crazy, messed up day.

And Kate had strolled in with her friends and hadn't come up to the bar once to speak to him. In the two weeks he'd given her space, he'd damn near lost his mind.

More orders flooded the system and Gray didn't slow down or stop. If Kate was here, then she was here to talk. She'd missed Ladies' Night last week and, like a fool, he'd watched the door. But he'd been so busy over the past fourteen days trying to get this place ready to sell that he'd let himself get wrapped up in the business.

He still hadn't made up his mind, but he had texted the guy and bought more time. Gray was inching closer to realizing he might never get a chance like this again. If he ever wanted to get out and see what he'd been missing in his life, now was the time.

What seemed like an eternity later, the crowd started winding down. Gray had caught glimpses of Kate, Lucy and Tara dancing, but now he only saw Kate in the corner booth alone and looking at something on her phone.

He left the bar to his employee and promised to be away only two minutes. Now that things weren't so insane, he wanted to talk to Kate.

As he crossed the bar, weaving through the tables and the stragglers who were still hanging out, Kate looked up and caught his gaze. Her eyes widened and with her tense shoulders and tight smile, Gray knew something was up.

Without asking, he slid into the booth across from her. "Didn't expect you to show up tonight."

She laid her phone in front of her and shrugged. "I needed to get out of the house. Plus, I needed to thank you for having Steven Sanders call me."

Gray eased back in the seat. "So he's on it. Good. I was giving him two more days to contact you before I called him again."

"He has other clients, you know."

Gray didn't care. What he cared about was helping Kate with her list and finding some sort of family for her to call her own.

"I hope he can find what you need," Gray replied.

Silence settled between them as she glanced down at her hands. She'd laced her fingers together and the way her knuckles were turning white made him wonder what was really on her mind.

"You're upset that I contacted him?" he guessed.

"No, no. I'm surprised and thankful," she corrected him.

"What's wrong?" he asked, leaning forward. "Lucy and Tara took off a while ago but you're still here."

Her eyes darted to the dancing women on the dance floor.

"Kate."

She turned her focus to him, but that didn't last long. Her gaze dropped once again to her clasped hands. "We need to talk. Can I wait until you're closed?"

Gray glanced to his watch. "We've got another hour. Do you want to go upstairs? You look like you could fall over."

And she did. She'd gone sans makeup, which wasn't unusual, but he could see the dark circles under her eyes, and she was a bit paler than normal.

"You feeling all right?" he asked.

She attempted a smile, but it was lame and forced. "Fine. I think I will go upstairs if you don't care. I can't leave without talking to you alone."

When she slid out of the booth, Gray came to his feet as well. She reached for the table with one hand and her head with the other as she teetered.

"Kate." He grasped her arms, holding tight. "I didn't make a drink for you. What have you had?"

She waved a hand away as she straightened. "I'm just tired and stood up too fast. I've only had water."

"Do you need something to eat?"

Shaking her head, she tried for a smile once again. "Really, I'm okay. I'll meet you upstairs when you're done."

He watched her head behind the bar and into the back hallway. Never in all his years as owner had he wanted to close up early and tell everyone to get the hell out.

Something was wrong with Kate. After all the running she'd done, something had pulled her back to him and he knew it wasn't the fact he'd called a genealogy specialist.

The next hour seemed to drag as he busted his butt to get the place ready to shut down for the night. He could sweep the floors and do a thorough wipe down in the morning. Once all the alcohol was taken care of, the kitchen was shut down properly and the employees were gone, Gray locked up and headed upstairs.

When he opened the door and stepped into the living room, he froze. There on his sofa was Kate all curled up in one corner. She'd removed her shoes and her little bare feet were tucked at her side.

She didn't look too comfortable at the angle her head had fallen against the back of the couch. Had she not been sleeping at home? Had she thought about his proposal and was here to…what? Take him up on it?

Gray turned the knob and slowly shut the door, careful not to click it into place. He crossed the room and took a seat directly in front of her on the old metal trunk he used as a coffee table. He watched her for a minute, torn between waking her and letting her get the sleep she seemed to desperately need.

After several minutes of feeling like a creeper, Gray reached out and tapped her leg. She didn't move. He flattened his hand around her thigh and gave a gentle squeeze.

"Kate," he said in a soft tone.

She started to stir. Her lids fluttered, then lifted. She blinked a few times as if focusing. Then she shot up on the sofa.

"Oh my gosh." Her hands immediately went to her hair, pushing wayward strands back from her face. "I didn't mean to fall asleep."

He held out his hands. "Relax. It's no big deal."

She swung her legs around and placed them on the area rug. The side of her knee brushed his as she propped her elbows on her thighs and rubbed her face.

"What's wrong, Kate?" He couldn't stand it any longer. "I gave you the space you asked for, but you show up here looking like a small gust of wind could blow you over. Are you sick? Don't lie to me."

Damn it, fear gripped him and he didn't like this feeling. Not one bit.

"I'm not sick." She dropped her hands in her lap and met his gaze dead-on. "I'm pregnant."

Chapter Fifteen

Kate stared at him, worried when the silence stretched longer than was comfortable.

She hadn't meant to just blurt that out, but honestly, was there a lead-in to such a bomb? Gray sat so close, their knees bumped. And for the second time in their years of friendship, she couldn't make out the expression on his face.

His eyes never wavered from her, but he reached out and gripped her hands in his. "Pregnant? Are you sure?"

Before she could answer, he shook his head. "That was stupid. You wouldn't tell me unless you were sure."

"I've suspected for a few days, but just took the test today."

Now his eyes did drop to her stomach. "I don't even know what to say. Are you... I mean, you feel okay?"

"I'm nauseous, tired, look like hell. Other than that, I'm fine."

Gray shifted his focus from her flat abdomen to her eyes. "You've never looked like hell in your life."

"You didn't see me hugging the commode this morning," she muttered.

His thumb raked over the back of her hand. "Did you come here to tell me you'd marry me?"

She'd been so afraid he'd say that. That he would just assume a baby would be a reason to marry. If the marriage wasn't going to be forever, how was joining lives the right thing to do?

"I'm not marrying you, Gray."

His dark brows drew in as he continued to stare at her. "Why not? This is all the more reason to get married. We're going to be parents. I can sell the bar, get the money, and we can go wherever you want. Hell, we'll travel and then decide where to settle down. Name it."

Kate shook her head and removed her hands from his. She leaned back on the couch and curled her feet back up beside her where they'd been.

"That's not the answer," she countered. "I don't want to keep doing this with you. We have time to figure out what the best plan will be for our baby."

"So if I sell the bar and leave, you'll what? Stay here? I want to be part of our child's life."

She knew he would. She expected him to be. Gray would be a wonderful father. He'd be a fabulous husband, just not in the way he was proposing. Literally.

"I'd never keep you away from the baby," she told him. "I'm hurt you would even suggest such a thing. If you leave, that's on you. I'll be right here in Stonerock."

He stared at her another minute and then finally pushed to his feet. "Stay here tonight," he said, looking down at her. "Just stay here so we can figure this out."

Kate smiled, but shook her head. "Sex isn't going to solve anything."

"Maybe I just want you here," he retorted. "Maybe I've missed you and now, knowing that you're carrying my child, I want to take care of you."

The tenderness in his voice warmed her. She knew he'd want to take over and make sure everything was perfect for her. He'd want to make her as comfortable as possible.

Unfortunately, through all of that, he just couldn't love her the way she wanted to be loved. The way she loved him.

Tears pricked her eyes. She dropped her head and brought her hands up to shield her face. Damn hormones.

"Kate." The cushion on the sofa sank next to her. One strong arm wrapped around her and she felt herself being pulled against his side. "Don't cry. Please. I'll figure something out."

Couldn't he see? This had nothing to do with the bar and if he kept it or sold it. If he loved her, truly loved her like a man loved a woman, she'd go anywhere with him. But she couldn't just uproot her life for a man who was settling and only trying to do the right thing.

"Stay," he whispered into her ear as he stroked her hair. "Sleeping. Nothing more."

She tipped her head back to peer up at him.

"Please."

She knew he only wanted to keep an eye on her, plus it was late and she was exhausted. Kate nodded. "I'll stay."

Gray left Kate sleeping and eased out of the bed. He glanced back down to where she lay wearing one of his shirts, her raven hair in a tangled mess around her, dark circles beneath her eyes. She'd been so exhausted when she'd come to the bar last night.

And she'd dropped the biggest bomb of his life.

A baby. He was having a baby with his best friend and she refused to marry him.

Gray had to convince her to. Before she'd changed his entire life with one sentence, he'd nearly talked himself into selling Gallagher's. Now that he knew he was going to be a father, well, he was sure he wanted to sell. He could use that money and make a nice life for his family...just as soon as he convinced

Kate to marry him. Didn't she see that this was the most logical step?

He hadn't planned on getting married, but with his dad always hinting that he should, with the new chapter of selling the bar, and with Kate pregnant... hell, he had to move forward with his plan and make her see this was the best option for their future.

Quietly he eased the door shut and went to the kitchen to make breakfast. He had no clue what was on her agenda today, but hopefully after a good night's sleep, they could talk and try to work things out. Well, he'd try to get her to see reason.

Gray checked his fridge and realized he hadn't been to the store in... Honestly, he couldn't remember the last time he went to the store.

He headed down to the bar and raided that kitchen, then ran back upstairs. Now he could actually start cooking something. Kate still slept, so he tried to be quiet. His apartment wasn't that big, but it worked for him.

That is, this space had always worked until now. He couldn't exactly expect Kate to raise a baby here. She valued family and the importance of home. Kate and the baby deserved a house with a yard, somewhere they could put a swing set. Something the total opposite of a bachelor pad above a bar.

Gray fried some potatoes he'd snagged from downstairs and pulled out the ham steaks from his freezer. Kate was more of a pancake girl, but she'd have to adapt today. He would see to it that she was cared for, whether she liked it or not.

He'd just dished up the plates when he heard running down the hall and then the bathroom door slamming shut.

Muttering a curse, he left the breakfast and went to the closed door. Yeah, she was definitely sick. He rubbed his hands down his face and stared up at the ceiling. How the hell could he make her feel better? He couldn't exactly fix this or take it from her.

He stood on the other side of the door and waited until the toilet flushed. He heard water running and, moments later, she opened the door. Gray hated how pale she was, how her hand shook as she shoved her hair away from her face.

"Sorry about that," she murmured, leaning against the door frame. "It hits quick."

He reached out and framed her face in his hands. "Never apologize to me. I made breakfast, but I'm thinking maybe you're not in the mood."

Her eyes shut as she wrinkled her nose. "Do you just have some juice?"

"Downstairs I do. I'll be right back."

In record time he had the juice and was racing back upstairs. As soon as he stepped into the apartment, he heard Kate talking.

"No, Chris. This isn't a good time."

Gray set the bottle on the small dining table and headed down the hall toward her voice. Chris, the bastard ex.

"I never agreed to meet up with you, so if you thought I did, then you're mistaken."

When Gray hit the doorway of his bedroom, he saw Kate sitting on the edge of his bed, her back to him. She had her head down and was rubbing it.

Anger bubbled within him. Who the hell was this guy who suddenly came back into her life? Why did he think she would want anything at all to do with him after the way he'd treated her?

"I don't care how long you're in town," she replied. "I'm busy."

She tapped the screen and tossed her cell on the bed.

"Has he been bothering you?" Gray asked, stepping into the room.

Kate turned to glance over her shoulder. "Just a few calls and texts. He only showed up at my house the one time."

If this jerk planned on staying in town, Gray intended to track him down. It was time for Chris to find out for good that he'd lost his chance at anything with Kate.

"I have your juice in the kitchen," he told her. "How are you feeling?"

She let out a slight laugh. "Confused. Scared. Powerless."

It probably wasn't the best time to tell her he felt the same way. Kate needed him to be strong, needed him to be there like he always had been. Even more so now.

Gray crossed the room and came to stand in front of her. "Don't answer me now, but think about marriage, Kate. There are so many reasons this is a good idea."

She stood, easing around him. "Not now, Gray. Just…not now."

"I'm just asking you to think about it."

He followed her down the hall to the kitchen. Grabbing a glass from the cabinet, he set it on the counter and poured her juice.

"I'm not asking for an answer today," he told her as she drank. "But you can't dismiss the idea completely."

She licked her lips and leveled her gaze. "Are you selling the bar?"

Gray swallowed, knowing he was going to have to say it out loud at some point. "Yes."

Kate pulled in a slow breath and nodded. Then she finished the last of the juice and handed him back the glass.

"Then go do what you need to do," she told him. "You wanted to figure out what your life was missing, and I sure as hell don't want to be the reason you stay. I won't be someone's burden and I won't let this baby feel that way, either."

Gray slammed the glass on the counter and took her by her shoulders. "You're not listening to me, damn it. You're not a burden, Kate. This baby isn't a burden. But selling the bar makes more sense now than ever. What? You want to live up here and raise a child?"

"We're not getting married or living together, so it's a moot point," she threw back at him. "I don't like this, Gray. We're always arguing and I just want my friend back."

Her voice cracked on that last word and he hauled her against his chest. He wanted his friend back, too, but they'd obliterated the friendship line and now they were adding a baby to the mix.

"We can't go back," he told her. "But I won't let you go through this alone. I'm here."

She eased back, piercing him with those blue eyes full of questions, but she asked only one.

"For how long?"

Chapter Sixteen

Well, there was no more dodging the inevitable.

Kate had asked the girls over since she knew Sam had Marley. This was definitely not a conversation for little ears.

She'd ordered pizza, made cookies, had wine and water on hand—everything was all set for the big reveal. Just then, her front door opened and Tara and Lucy came in, chattering.

Kate heard Lucy saying something about her stepdaughter, but couldn't make out exactly what it was. When she'd married Noah, she'd gotten an instant family and was filling the role of mom beautifully. Tara excelled at motherhood, despite the roller coaster she'd had to endure these past several months with Sam and his addiction.

Looked like Kate couldn't have asked for two better women to call on for support. She only hoped they weren't too angry with her for keeping the situation with Gray a secret.

Kate stepped from the kitchen into the living room. "Hey, guys."

"I smell pizza," Tara stated. "Please, tell me you got extra bacon on at least part of it."

Kate rolled her eyes. "Have I ever let you down? I even bought your favorite wine, though wine and pizza always sounded like a bad combo to me."

Lucy set her purse on the accent chair and dropped her keys inside. "Wine goes with everything and so does pizza, so it only makes sense to pair them together."

Kate attempted a smile, but her nerves were spiraling out of control. She could do this. There was nothing to be afraid of and her friends would be there for her. Isn't that what they did? They banded together during the best and worst of times.

"Oh, no." Tara took a slow step forward. "I thought we were just having a random girls' night. What's wrong, Kate?"

"You guys might want to sit down with a glass of wine first."

Lucy crossed her arms over her chest and shook her head. "Not until you tell us what's wrong."

"Nothing is wrong, exactly," she replied. "Gray and I—"

"Finally." Tara threw her hands in the air. "I knew something was going on with the two of you. What is it, though? You seem, I don't know...nervous."

"Are you and Gray together?" Lucy whispered as if this was some sacred secret.

"You could say that."

Kate looked from one friend to the other. They'd barely made it inside the front door, and from the determined look on their faces, they weren't moving any further until she confessed.

"I'm pregnant."

Tara's eyes widened. Lucy's mouth dropped. Neither said a word, but their shock spoke volumes.

"We were just fooling around," Kate went on. "I mean, there was the night of the rehearsal dinner, then camping—"

"I called this," Tara repeated. "Well, not the baby. Damn, Kate. You're having a baby?"

Kate couldn't help the smile and shrug. "Of all people, the CEO of Savvy Scheduler did not plan this."

Lucy stepped forward and extended her arms. Kate shook her head and held her hands out, silently telling her friend no.

"I can't do comfort right now," she explained. "I'm barely hanging on here and I just need to come to grips with this—"

Lucy wrapped her arms around Kate and that was

all it took for Kate to finally crumble. Tears fell, fear took hold, and soon Tara's arms were banding around them as well.

"It's going to be okay," Tara stated. "A baby is a wonderful blessing."

"What did Gray say?" Lucy asked, easing back slightly.

Kate sniffed and attempted to gather herself together. "He proposed," she whispered.

"That's great," Tara exclaimed. "I always thought you two would end up together."

Swiping her face with the back of her hand, Kate pulled in a shaky breath. "I turned him down."

Tara gripped her shoulder. "What?"

"I'm not settling," Kate explained. "I want to marry someone who loves me, who isn't marrying me because of some family pressure or a pregnancy."

Kate stepped back to get some space. She didn't want to cry about this, didn't want pity. She wanted to figure out what her next step should be and she needed to be logical about it.

Maneuvering around her friends, who continued to stare at her as if she'd break again, Kate went to the sofa and sank into the corner.

"He proposed before I told him about the baby," she explained. "He's got that offer to sell the bar and his father has been on him for years to settle down. Gray wants to move ahead with the deal and figured if we got married, maybe his dad wouldn't be so upset about losing Gallagher's. Then when I told him about the baby, well, he thinks it's only logical."

Tara sat on the edge of the accent chair across from the sofa. "What's logical is that you should tell him how you really feel so the two of you can move on."

"You do love him, right?" Lucy asked as she sat in the chair right next to Tara's hip. "I don't mean like you love us as your friends. I mean, you love Gray. I know you do or you never would've slept with him."

Kate couldn't deny it—she didn't want to. She was tired of the sneaking, the secrets, the emotions.

"I do," she whispered. "But it's irrelevant because he doesn't see me like that."

"Men are blind." Lucy reached over to pat Kate's knee. "Sometimes you have to bang them over the head in order for them to see the truth. You need to be honest with Gray. He should know how you feel."

Kate had put her love out there before. She'd had a ring on her finger and a dress in her closet, but that love—or what she'd thought was love—had been thrown back in her face.

She loved Gray more than she ever did Chris. Gray was…well, he was everything. How would she handle it if he rejected her? At least if she kept her feelings locked inside her heart, they could remain friends, raise the baby and not muddle up their relationship with one-sided love.

"How are you feeling, other than Gray?" Tara asked. "Physically, I mean. Have you been sick?"

"Gray made me potatoes and ham for breakfast and the smell woke me when my stomach started rolling. Sick doesn't begin to describe my mornings."

Lucy's eyes widened. "He made you breakfast? That's so sweet."

Kate laughed. "He's always taken care of me. That's not the problem."

"The key to any good relationship is communication," Tara stated, and the wistfulness in her tone had Kate turning her focus on her. "Trust me. You need to tell him how you feel."

Kate tucked her hair behind her ears and wondered what would be best. Baring her heart to Gray as to her true feelings or just waiting to see what happened? For all she knew, he would sell the bar, go on some grand adventure to find himself and then discover that he never wanted to return. Then what?

"I honestly don't know what to do," she muttered. "I don't want him to feel sorry for me or think I fell in love with him because of the pregnancy. I've loved him… I don't even know how long. Maybe forever, but I didn't realize it until recently."

Lucy grabbed Kate's hand. "Well, right now let's focus on you and this baby. I'm confident Gray will come around."

Kate wished she had Lucy's confidence and Tara's courage. But this was her life and this pregnancy was the biggest thing that had ever happened to her. And she didn't want to put her heart on the line again because she'd been right from the very beginning. She could lose Gray's friendship if all of this went wrong. Losing the one constant man in her life wasn't an option. Especially now that the same man would be needed as a constant for their baby.

Gray set the glass of sweet tea on the counter in front of Sam. The bar didn't open for another hour and Sam had stopped by after a long week at his new job. Gray admired the man for putting his family first, for selling his own company and humbling himself to get counseling before going to work for another construction company.

He'd helped himself but may never get his wife back. The harsh reality was a bitch to bear, Gray was sure. Sam was a great guy who'd made poor decisions.

"Are you really selling the bar?" Sam asked, gripping the frosted glass.

Gray flattened his palms on the rolled edge of the bar. "I am. I haven't contacted the guy from Knoxville yet, but I plan on calling Monday morning."

"What does your dad say about it?"

Gray didn't like to think of the disappointment he'd seen in his father's eyes. He knew his dad wanted to keep the bar in the family, but would ultimately support Gray no matter what.

The problem was, Gray wasn't a hundred percent sure what he wanted. He did know that the money from the sale would put him in a perfect spot to provide for Kate and the baby.

He hadn't mentioned the baby to his dad because that would've brought up a whole other set of issues…like the fact that she wouldn't marry him.

But he knew where her doubts were coming from. Kate had been left so shaken when her parents had passed. Then her fiancé had revealed his true colors and broken her heart. Gray never wanted her to question where her foundation was again. He knew she was scared with this pregnancy—hell, he was, too. But there was nothing he wouldn't do for her even if she refused to marry him.

"Dad isn't happy," Gray finally replied. "But he respects my decision. He'd like to see me settled down with a wife and a bunch of little Gallaghers running around and gearing up to pass this place to them."

Sam took a hearty drink of his tea and set the glass back down. "That's not what you want, I take it."

Gray gave a slight shrug, feeling something tug on his heart. "I don't know what I want, but has been on my mind."

Especially now.

"It's not for everyone, that's for sure." Sam slid his thumb over the condensation of his mug. "Tara is everything and when you find a love like that, it's worth fighting for. I really messed up, Gray. Don't learn from my mistakes."

Gray gritted his teeth and tried to sort through the thoughts scrolling through his head.

The most dominant thought was love. Love worth fighting for. He loved Kate. Hadn't he told her as much? They'd loved each other for years, so why was she so adamant about not marrying him? Wasn't any level of love a good basis for a marriage?

But she'd told him she wouldn't settle, that she wanted to be with a man who loved her the way a husband should love his wife.

He didn't even know what that meant. He thought she'd be happy with him, that they could be happy together. Obviously she had other expectations about her future.

"How are things with Tara?" Gray asked.

Sam shrugged. "Still the same. We get along for Marley and we're always civil, but it seems so shallow, you know? We just go through the days, same cycle, same fake smiles, like we're both not hurting."

Gray hated seeing his friends so torn. Yes, Sam had made mistakes, but he was human and he'd fought like hell to get clean and make up for the pain he'd caused.

Is this how Gray and Kate would be? Would they be moving through the days just living civilly and trying not to break? Would they bounce their child back and forth and pretend everything was okay?

And what would happen if Kate wanted to go on a date or brought a man home?

Jealousy spiraled through him at the mere thought of another man in Kate's life. Another man in their child's life.

Gray went about getting the bar ready to open. He chatted with his employees when they came in the back door and he welcomed the first customers who started to filter in. Sam remained on his stool, sipping his tea, then finally beer. Gray made sure to always keep an eye on his friend when he came in, and Sam usually limited his drinking to one or two beers. He seemed to be on the road to getting his life back under control.

Too bad Gray couldn't say the same.

Chapter Seventeen

"This was a mistake," Kate growled as Lucy practically dragged her inside the front door of Gallagher's. "A pregnant woman shouldn't be hanging out at the bar."

Lucy held onto her arm. "This is exactly where that pregnant lady should be when the man she loves is the owner. Besides, Tara is home with Marley tonight and Noah took Piper on a father-daughter date to the movies. I wanted to get out, so you're stuck with me."

Kate shouldn't be here. Then again, she shouldn't have put on her favorite dress and curled her hair, either. She didn't do those things for Gray. Absolutely not. She did them for herself because…

Fine. She did them for Gray because no matter how much she wished it, she couldn't just move on and forget her feelings for him. Pregnancy aside, Kate wanted Gray just as much as ever. Even if she hadn't been carrying his child, she would be completely in love with him.

For years she'd wanted a family of her own. She'd dreamed of it, in fact. Then she'd started her little business and focused on that after her world was rocked when Chris left. Now she was being given a second chance at a family, but Gray wasn't on board...not in the way she needed him to be.

Inside Gallagher's, an upbeat country song was blasting as several couples danced. The tables were full, except for one table right smack-dab in the middle of the floor. Fabulous. Why couldn't their usual corner booth be open? That real estate should always be on reserve for her.

Kate dropped to the hard wooden seat and hung her purse on the back. This was not ideal, not at all. Here she was, front and center of the bar, almost as if fate was mocking her.

A slow, twangy song filled the space and even more couples flooded to the dance floor.

"Fancy seeing you here."

Kate turned around, barely registering the cheesy line and her ex before he whisked her out of her seat and spun her toward the dance floor.

In a blur, she saw Lucy's shocked face.

"Chris, what in the world," she said, trying to

wriggle free of his grip on her hand. "I don't want to dance."

Banding an arm around her waist, he took her free hand in his and maneuvered them right into the midst of the dancers.

"Just one dance," he said, smiling down at her as if he had every right to hold her. "Surely you can give me three minutes to talk and then I'll leave you alone."

Kate didn't want to give him three seconds, let alone three minutes. She didn't get a chance to say anything because Chris was jerked from her and then Gray stood towering over him.

"You're Chris?" Gray asked, his body taut with tension.

Kate stepped forward and put her hand on his back. "Don't, Gray."

Ignoring her, he took a half step forward, causing Chris to shove at Gray. "I'm talking to Kate, if you don't mind."

"I actually do mind," Gray growled over the music. A crowd had formed around them.

"It's fine," Kate insisted. She didn't want an altercation.

"You heard the lady," Chris said with a smirk. "It's fine. Now go back to making drinks."

Kate didn't have time to react as Gray's fist drew back and landed right in the middle of Chris's face. Her ex stumbled back, landing on a table and upending another one.

Gray shook his hand out and Kate stepped around to stand in front of him, worried he'd go at Chris again. The last thing Gray needed was to get in a fight in his own bar. That wouldn't be good for business.

"Stop it," she demanded.

The look on his face was pure fury. Finally, he took his gaze from Chris and landed it on her. "Keep your boyfriend out of my bar."

Kate drew her brows in and dropped her hand. "What is wrong with you?"

"What the hell?"

Kate turned around to see some guy helping Chris up. The stranger turned his attention to Gray. "This is how you run a business?"

Gray moved around Kate and walked past Chris, the stranger and the crowd. Kate stared at his retreating back and was startled when a hand fell on her shoulder. She spun around to find Lucy.

"That was…territorial."

Kate shook her head. "What just happened?"

"I'd say your guy got jealous, but who was the other man who stepped in?"

Gray stalked back over to Chris and the other man. Kate watched, waiting and hoping there wasn't going to be another altercation.

"The bar isn't for sale." Gray stood directly in front of the two guys. Chris held his jaw, working it back and forth. "You two can get the hell out of here and don't come back."

Gray and Chris sparring wasn't something she thought she'd ever see. But no doubt about it, Chris wasn't going to win this fight no matter what he threatened.

"I'll sue you," Chris spouted. "My partner and I were going to give you a lot of money for this place."

"Sue me," Gray said, crossing his arms over his massive chest as if he didn't have a care in the world. "But leave."

He turned back around and went back to the bar. Kate watched as he started making drinks like his whole life hadn't just changed. Chris was a bastard, no doubt about it.

He'd wanted to sell the bar. He'd been pretty set on doing just that. What had changed his mind? He hadn't said a word to her. Between Gray's silence and Chris's betrayal, Kate wasn't sure how to feel, but pissed was a great starting point.

Then dread filled her. Had he done this because of the baby? Was he giving up what he truly wanted to make her happy? Because he'd done that with his father, when he'd taken over the bar after his tour of duty just to appease him. And here he was putting his own needs aside again. Kate intended to find out why.

Chris and his business partner turned and left, leaving many talking about what had just happened. Obviously the other guy was the one who'd made Gray the exorbitant offer.

"I can't believe he just hit him," Kate muttered.

Lucy laughed. "I recall him hitting another guy who got in your face several months ago."

Kate ran a hand through her hair as she met Gray's dark eyes across the bar. "At least he's consistent."

"Heard you made a little scene at the bar last night."

Gray rubbed his eyes and attempted to form a coherent sentence. His father had called way too early, knowing full well that Gray would still be asleep. The man had run the same bar for thirty years. He knew the routine.

"Nothing I couldn't handle."

Gray eased up in bed and leaned against the headboard because he knew his father didn't randomly call just to chat.

"Also heard you turned down the offer to sell."

Gray blew out a breath. Yeah. He had. That hadn't been an easy decision, but definitely the right one. The second he'd seen Kate in another man's arms, Gray had lost it. Then, on his way over, he'd heard Kate call the guy Chris and Gray nearly exploded. Okay, he did explode, but that guy deserved the punch—and more—for what he'd done years ago.

Kate was his family. Kate and their child was his family. The future had seemed so clear in that moment. All the times he'd waited for a sign, waited for some divine intervention to tell him what to do. But Kate and their family was everything. And he'd found that he wanted to continue that tradition with his child, boy or girl.

"I'm keeping the bar," Gray confirmed.

"Who changed your mind?" his dad asked.

Gray instantly pictured Kate. He couldn't help but smile though he was dead tired. He'd screwed up things with her. He'd legit botched up their relationship from the friendship to the intimacy. But he had a plan.

"I just realized nothing is missing from my life," Gray replied. "I'm staying here and Gallagher's will remain in the family."

"That was a lot of money to turn down, son."

Funny, but that didn't bother him anymore. "It was," he agreed. "Family means more."

Family meant *everything*.

He needed to tell his dad about the pregnancy, but he wanted to talk to Kate first. He had quite a bit to talk to her about, actually.

"I'm proud of you," his dad finally said. "Your grandfather would be, too, knowing you decided to stay in Stonerock, keep the tradition alive."

A lump formed in Gray's throat. "I wouldn't be anywhere else."

"Well, I guess I'll let you get back to sleep," his dad chuckled. "But Gray. Let's lay off the hitting. I know you have a thing for Kate, but control yourself."

His dad hung up before Gray could say anything about Kate or his self-control. He tossed his phone onto the rumpled sheet next to his hip. Raking his hands over his face, Gray attempted to sort his thoughts, his plans. Today he was taking back his life. Taking what he'd always wanted, but never knew he was missing.

And Kate wasn't going to get away again.

Chapter Eighteen

She hadn't seen Gray since the night before last. He'd punched Chris, turned down an enormous business deal and gone back to brooding.

Out of the blue, he'd texted this morning to tell her she'd left something at his apartment. There was no way she'd left anything there because she was meticulous about her stuff and knew where everything was.

Clearly he wanted her there for another reason. Kate found herself sipping her ginger ale and clutching a cracker as she mounted the outside back steps to the bar apartment.

Shoving the rest of the cracker in her mouth, she gripped the knob and eased the door open.

"Gray?" she called out as she stepped inside.

She'd never knocked before, so she didn't now, plus he knew she was coming.

Kate stepped into the living area and stopped short. The picture over the sofa was no longer the tacky *Dogs Playing Poker*. Tears pricked her eyes as she stepped closer to the image, one she'd seen so many times, but never like this.

A young Kate stared back at her. On either side of her in the portrait were her parents. All three smiling, not knowing what the future held. Kate had this exact picture in her bedroom.

"You like it?"

Kate was startled as Gray's easy question pulled her from the moment. Without turning, she nodded. Emotions formed heavy in her throat as her eyes burned with unshed tears.

"I remember that day so vividly," she told him, taking in every feature of her parents' faces. "We'd just gone for a picnic at one of the state parks. Then Dad took us on a small hike. My mom tripped on a rock and tore a hole in her tennis shoe. We laughed because she was always so clumsy."

She could still hear her mother's laugh—so sweet, almost wistful. "Not a day goes by that I don't miss them."

"They'd be proud of you."

Kate smiled as she turned to face Gray. "I hope so. I wonder what they'd think of me becoming a mother. Not having mine right now is…"

She blew out a breath and tried to gather her thoughts.

"I'm sure it's difficult," he told her as he remained in the doorway to the bedroom. "My mother passed when I was little, so I don't remember her. You're going to be a great mother and you've got those fond memories that will help."

She met his gaze, biting her bottom lip to cease the quivering.

"And you've got me," he added.

Kate blinked away the moisture and turned back to look at the picture. "Why is this hanging here?" she asked.

"This is your birthday present. It didn't come in on time, but I want you to have it."

This is what he'd done for her. For years he'd given her chocolate-covered strawberries, and this year had been no different. But he'd gone a step further and done something so thoughtful, so unique. Damn it, why did love have to be a one-way street with him?

"How did you get a copy?" she asked.

"Social media. I pulled it from one of your accounts and had it blown up on the canvas."

Crossing her arms, Kate turned her attention back to Gray. "If it's my birthday present, why is it hanging here?"

"Because you didn't like the other painting."

Confused, Kate shook her head. "I don't understand."

Gray pushed off the doorway and closed the distance between them. He stood directly in front of her, within touching distance, but didn't reach for her. As she studied the fine lines around his eyes, she realized he was tired. Had he not slept lately? Was he regretting his decision not to sell the bar?

"You and this baby are my priority now," he stated simply. "Not the bar, not moving and taking that money. Nothing else matters but my family."

What? Did he mean…

"I don't care where we take the picture I got you," he went on. "If you want to live here, we leave it here. You want to stay in your house, we hang it there. Our child will know your parents and I want to create a family with you."

"Gray," she whispered.

She dropped her face to her hands as another wave of emotions overcame her. He was only saying this to appease his dad, to make his father see that Gray was ready to settle down.

Kate swiped her face and met Gray's eyes. "We've been over this."

Now he did reach for her. Those large, strong hands framed her face. "No, we haven't, because we're about to have a whole new conversation. I need your undivided attention when I tell you I'm in love with you."

Kate's heart clenched. She stared up at him, gripped his wrists, and murmured, "You—you're in love with me? As in…"

"As in I want to make you my wife, not because of the baby and not because I'm staying here and keeping the bar." A ghost of a smile formed on his lips. "All these years I thought there was a void, but there wasn't. You were here all along and the only thing missing was having you even deeper in my life. That was the void. I need you, Kate. I know you'd be fine without me and we could share joint custody of our baby, but I want this life with you. I want this child and more with you."

Tears spilled and there was no way she could even think of holding them back. "You're serious?"

Gray laughed, then nipped at her lips. "You think I'd get rid of my dog picture for just anybody? I love you, Kate. I love this baby."

"But you were so angry the other night and I thought…"

"I wasn't angry with you," he assured her. "I was angry with that jerk who held you in his arms. I was angry with myself for being a dick to you, for not realizing sooner exactly how much you mean to me."

Gripping his wrists tighter, she so hoped he meant that. Every part of her wanted him to love her, to love this baby and to want to be a united family.

"Are you sure this isn't because of the baby?" she repeated.

"It's because of us," he stated, swiping the moisture from her cheeks. "If you weren't pregnant, I'd still be in love with you. I'd still want to spend my life with you."

"Spend your life with me?"

Gray let out a soft chuckle as he stepped back and dropped his hands. "You keep answering me with questions."

Kate watched as he went to the bedroom and came out a moment later holding something behind his back.

"I got something else for you."

Honestly, she wasn't sure how much more she could take. Between the photo and the declaration of love, she had more than she'd ever wanted.

Gray pulled out a thick book from behind his back. No. It wasn't a book at all.

Kate busted out laughing. "A planner?"

Gray got down on one knee and her breath caught in her throat. "Not just any planner, babe. Our life starts now. Marry me."

The front of the planner had a big gold heart on a white background. Gray opened the cover to reveal an attached satin ribbon to use for marking pages.

"Gray," she gasped.

Tied to the satin ribbon was a ring.

"I was just going to propose with the planner because I realize that's more important than jewelry to you," he joked. "But I hope you'll take this ring. It was my mother's. My dad saved it for me to give to the woman I love. There's nobody else I would ever give this ring to."

Kate's nausea chose that moment to make an appearance. She swayed on her feet, and Gray instantly came to his and wrapped an arm around her waist.

"I hope that's the baby and not my proposal," he said, guiding her to the couch.

"Definitely the baby," she told him.

He set the planner down on the old, antique trunk. "What can I get you?"

Kate closed her eyes, willing the dizziness to pass. "The ring on my finger, for starters."

She risked looking over at him and found him smiling, his eyes misting. "Are you going to cry?" she asked.

"Me? No. I don't cry." He sniffed as he untied the ring and held it up to her. "My dad said my mom loved pearls, but if you want a diamond or, hell... I don't know. I'll get anything, Kate. I just want you."

She held out her left hand. "And I want you and this ring that means so much to you."

Gray slid the ring onto her finger and let out a breath. "I so hoped this would fit."

Kate extended her arm and admired the ring. "It's perfect."

He pulled her into his arms. "We're perfect. I'm sorry I didn't see this before. When you said you needed me to love you like you deserve, I didn't get it."

Kate slid her arm around his abdomen and toed off her sandals. She propped her feet on the trunk and nestled deeper into his side.

"I've always loved you," he went on. "I even loved

you like a husband should love a wife, but it took a reality check for me to fully realize it."

"Was it Chris coming back to town?"

"Part of it," he replied, trailing his fingertips up and down her arm. "When you weren't here, I felt empty. Once we slept together that first time, everything changed. I wanted you more and more, not just for the sex, but because I felt alone without you."

Kate smiled and eased up. "Then you took me camping to seduce me."

A naughty grin spread across his face. "I took you camping to mark an item off your bucket list. The seducing was just a handy by-product."

His face sobered as he studied her. "I meant what I said before about helping you fulfill your list. Have you heard any more from the genealogy expert?"

"Not yet, but he's starting his research and that's a step in the right direction."

Gray kissed the tip of her nose. "What do you say we go pick out that dog you wanted? Sprout, right?"

Her eyes widened. "Right now?"

With a shrug, Gray sat up. "Why not? The local shelter is open."

Of course he'd want a shelter dog. As if the man couldn't be more perfect. She reached out and fisted his unruly hair in her hands, pulling his mouth down to hers.

"You're so perfect," she muttered against his lips. "Let's go get our Sprout."

"Want to get married, too?"

Kate stilled. "Today?"

"You still looking for something spontaneous for your list?"

The planner inside her started to have anxiety, but the woman who stared at this man wanted him to be hers in every single way.

"Don't worry about the perfect venue or the gown or flowers," he told her. "Marry me, Kate. Now. Today."

She let out a laugh, completely shocked at her response. "Let's do it."

Gray lifted her up into his arms and held her tight. There was no one else on earth who could make her want to ignore her plans and throw caution to the wind. But Gray made her want to live in the moment.

"Maybe I should write this in my planner," she told him.

He set her down on her feet and smiled as he reached down to flip the pages of the planner. "I already did. I had a feeling you'd say yes."

Kate glanced at the open pages. Her heart leaped in her chest at Gray's writing on today's date: Making Kate My Wife.

She smacked a kiss on his cheek. "I'm going to turn you into a personal planner after all."

"As long as you're mine, I'll make a thousand lists with you."

Epilogue

Sam stood outside his front door. Well, not *his* front door, since he and Tara had separated. Everyone thought their divorce was final and he'd never said otherwise. Tara had wanted the divorce, and he deserved all of her anger, but he'd never signed the papers. Sam Bailey never gave up and he sure as hell didn't intend to now—even when his entire world was slipping from his grasp.

He tapped his knuckles on the door—a door he'd installed when they'd bought the house only three years ago, a door he'd walked through thousands of times without thinking twice. Those days were gone. He'd severed his right to just walk in. At this point, he just hoped Tara talked to him.

The dead bolt flicked and Tara eased the door open, pulling her robe tighter around her chest.

"Sam, what are you doing here?"

She always looked gorgeous. Whether she wore her ratty old bathrobe or she had on a formfitting dress. His Tara was a complete knockout. Only she wasn't his anymore.

"Marley called me."

"What?"

"She said you'd been crying." He studied her face but didn't notice any traces of tears. "Everything okay?"

"I wasn't crying," she stated, but her swollen, red eyes gave her away. "Nothing for you to worry about. What else did she tell you?"

Sam swallowed. This wasn't the first time Marley had called him, trying to find a reason to get him to come over. He knew his little girl wanted her parents to live together again, but it just wasn't possible right now.

Even so, he and Tara had made it clear they would put Marley first at all times. They didn't want her to suffer any more than necessary. Keeping her happy, feeling secure, was top of their priority list.

"I'm fine." Tara licked her lips and raked a hand through her hair, then opened the door wider. "Do you want to come in and see her? She's getting ready for bed. Or I thought she was. I'm sorry. I had no idea she called you."

Again.

The word hovered between them because this wasn't the first time, and likely not the last. But Sam would come every single time if there was the slightest chance something was wrong with Tara.

"I shouldn't come in." Though he desperately wanted to. He wanted to walk in that door and tuck his daughter into bed and then go to his own room with his wife. "I don't want her to think she can keep doing this when there's nothing wrong."

But there was so much that was wrong. So much pain, so much heartache. All of it caused by his selfish desires, his addiction. An addiction he'd put ahead of his own family.

Tara glanced over her shoulder, then eased out the front door and closed it at her back. Sam adjusted his stance to make room for her. The glow of the porch lights illuminated her green eyes. It was those wide, expressive eyes that had initially drawn him to her.

"I know you're trying to move forward, to seek forgiveness or even more from me." She looked down to her clasped hands and shook her head. "But you can't keep leaving notes, Sam."

That's how he'd originally started to get her attention when he was serious about dating her. Stonerock was a small town, so they'd known each other for years, but something had shifted. He'd leave random notes asking her out and then, once they were together all the time, he'd leave little love notes. He'd done that for years, wanting her to know how special she was.

He'd messed up. There was no denying the facts. All he could do now was try to prove to her, to Marley that he was the man they needed him to be. No matter how long it took.

"I'm a patient man," he told her, fisting his hands at his sides because he wanted to reach out and touch her. He wanted to brush her hair back from her face and feel the silkiness of her skin once more. "I know I hurt you. I know I hurt Marley. But you know me, babe. I'm going to make this right."

"It's over," she whispered. "I don't want to keep dragging this out. What happened is in the past and we both need to move forward. It's not healthy, Sam."

"No, it's not," he agreed. "I'm starting over, Tara. I'm trying one day at a time."

"Maybe you should just sign the papers," she whispered through her emotion as she went back inside.

The door closed. The click of the lock seemed to echo in the dark of the night. But Sam couldn't give up. His family needed him.

He had every intention of proving to Tara that he could be a better man.

* * * * *

*Don't miss any of the stories
set in Stonerock, Tennessee!
Only from Jules Bennett!*

*Dr. Daddy's Perfect Christmas
The Fireman's Ready-Made Family
From Best Friend to Bride
The Cowboy's Second-Chance Family
From Best Friend to Daddy*

COMING NEXT MONTH FROM

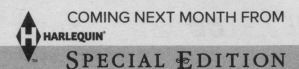

HARLEQUIN®

SPECIAL EDITION

Available April 17, 2018

#2617 THE NANNY'S DOUBLE TROUBLE
The Bravos of Valentine Bay • by Christine Rimmer
Despite their family connection, Keely Ostergard and Daniel Bravo have never gotten along. But when Keely steps in as emergency nanny to Daniel's twin toddlers, she quickly finds herself sweet on the single dad.

#2618 MADDIE FORTUNE'S PERFECT MAN
The Fortunes of Texas: The Rulebreakers
by Nancy Robards Thompson
When Maddie Fortunado's father announces that she and Zach McCarter—Maddie's secret office crush—are competing to be his successor, Maddie's furious. But as they work together to land a high-profile listing, they discover an undeniable chemistry and a connection that might just pull each of them out of the fortifications they've built to protect their hearts.

#2619 A BACHELOR, A BOSS AND A BABY
Conard County: The Next Generation • by Rachel Lee
Diane Finch is fostering her cousin's baby and can't find suitable day care. In steps her boss, Blaine Harrigan, who loves kids and just wants to help. As they grow closer, will the secret Diane is keeping be the thing that tears them apart?

#2620 HER WICKHAM FALLS SEAL
Wickham Falls Weddings • by Rochelle Alers
Teacher Taryn Robinson leaves behind a messy breakup and moves to a small town to become former navy SEAL Aiden Gibson's young daughters' tutor. Little does she know she's found much more than a job—she's found a family!

#2621 THE LIEUTENANTS' ONLINE LOVE
American Heroes • by Caro Carson
Thane Carter and Chloe Michaels are both lieutenants in the same army platoon—and they butt heads constantly. Luckily, they have their online pen pals to vent to. Until Thane finds out the woman he's starting to fall for is none other than the workplace rival he's forbidden to date!

#2622 REUNITED WITH THE SHERIFF
The Delaneys of Sandpiper Beach • by Lynne Marshall
Shelby and Conor promised to meet on the beach two years after the best summer of their lives, but when Shelby never showed, Conor's heart was shattered. Now she's back in Sandpiper Beach and working at his family's hotel. Can Conor let the past go long enough to see if they can finally find forever?

YOU CAN FIND MORE INFORMATION ON UPCOMING HARLEQUIN® TITLES, FREE EXCERPTS AND MORE AT WWW.HARLEQUIN.COM.

HSECNM0418

Get 2 Free Books,
Plus 2 Free Gifts—
just for trying the Reader Service!

HARLEQUIN

SPECIAL EDITION

But Thane took only one more step before stopping, watching in horror as Michaels entered row D from the other side. Good God, what were the odds? This was ridiculous. It was the biggest night of his life, the night when he was finally going to meet the woman of his dreams, and Michaels was here to make it all difficult.

He retreated. He backed out of the row and went back up a few steps, row E, row F, going upstream against the flow of people. He paused there. He'd let Michaels take her seat, then he'd go back in and be careful not to look toward her end of the row as he took his seat in the center. If he didn't make eye contact, he wouldn't have to acknowledge her existence at all.

He watched Michaels pass seat after seat after seat, smiling and nodding thanks as she worked her way into the row, his horror growing as she got closer and closer to the center of the row, right to where he and Ballerina were going to meet.

No.

Michaels was wearing black, not pink and blue. It was a freak coincidence that she was standing in the center of the row. She'd probably entered from the wrong side and would keep moving to this end, to a seat near his aisle.

The house lights dimmed halfway. Patrons started hustling toward their seats in earnest. Michaels stayed where she was, right in the center, and sat down.

Thane didn't move as the world dropped out from under him.

Then anger propelled him. Thane turned to walk up a few more rows. He didn't want Michaels to see him. He'd wait, out of the way, until he saw Ballerina show up, because Michaels was not, could not be, Ballerina.

He stomped up to row G. Row H.

Not. Possible.

There'd been some mistake. Thane turned around and leaned his back against the wall, leaving room for others to continue past him. He focused fiercely on the row closest to the railing. That was A. The next one back was B, then C, and…D. No mistake. Michaels was sitting in D. In the center.

He glared daggers at the back of her head, hating all those tendrils and curls and flowers. His heart contracted hard in his chest; those flowers in her hair were pink and blue.

Ballerina was Michaels.

Don't miss
THE LIEUTENANTS' ONLINE LOVE by Caro Carson,
available May 2018 wherever
Harlequin® Special Edition books and ebooks are sold.

www.Harlequin.com

New York Times bestselling author

BRENDA NOVAK

returns to Fairham Island with another exciting, emotional and intense romantic thriller.

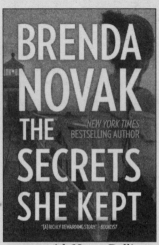

The rich and powerful Josephine Lazarow, matriarch of Fairham Island, is dead. The police say it's suicide, but Keith, her estranged son, doesn't believe it.

After walking away from his mother and her controlling ways five years ago, he's built a new life in LA.

Problem is...coming home to Fairham puts him back in contact with Nancy Dellinger, the woman he hurt so badly when he left before. And digging that deep into his mother's final days and hours entails a very real risk. Because the person who killed her could be someone he loves...

Available now, wherever books are sold.